Katie

starting from scratch

This book is a work of fiction. Any references to historical events, real people, or real places are used fictitiously. Other names, characters, places, and events are products of the author's imagination, and any resemblance to actual events or places or persons, living or dead, is entirely coincidental.

SIMON SPOTLIGHT
An imprint of Simon & Schuster Children's Publishing Division
1230 Avenue of the Americas, New York, New York 10020
Copyright © 2014 by Simon & Schuster, Inc.
All rights reserved, including the right of reproduction
in whole or in part in any form.
SIMON SPOTLIGHT and colophon are registered
trademarks of Simon & Schuster, Inc.
Text by Tracey West
Chapter header illustrations by Maryam Choudhury
Designed by Laura Roode
For information about special discounts for bulk purchases, please contact
Simon & Schuster Special Sales at 1-866-506-1949
or business@simonandschuster.com.
Manufactured in the United States of America 1020 SKY
First Edition 4 6 8 10 9 7 5 3
ISBN 978-1-4814-0471-6 (pbk)
ISBN 978-1-4814-0472-3 (hc)
ISBN 978-1-4814-0473-0 (eBook)
Library of Congress Control Number 2014939568

CUPCAKE DIARIES

Katie

starting
from
scratch

by coco simon

Simon Spotlight

New York   London   Toronto   Sydney   New Delhi

Katie

CHAPTER 1

Really, Mom?

So, Emily, what's new with you? How are things going at school?" my mom asked the girl sitting next to me.

"It's okay," Emily replied. "I like all my teachers."

Emily's dad, who was sitting next to my mom, smiled at her.

I should probably remind you that Emily's dad, Jeff, is also a math teacher at the middle school that I go to. There I call him "Mr. Green." And Jeff, or Mr. Green or whatever you want to call him, happens to be dating my mom. It gets a little awkward sometimes to have your mom dating a teacher at school, but I'm dealing with it.

"Have you ever had trouble with the lock on your locker?" Mom asked Emily. Mom nodded toward me. "Katie had a hard time getting the hang of it. Once she even called me at work because she couldn't get it open."

I looked at my mom in disbelief. "Really, Mom? Do you have to tell everybody that?"

Maybe normally I would have just laughed at a comment about that (especially since Mom was right), but lately Mom was doing this thing with Emily, like sort of selling me out to get closer to her, that was starting to get annoying. And even more stuff happened during our dinner that night at the Maple Grove Diner.

Mom changed the subject of my un-awesome lock-opening ability—but the conversation didn't get any better.

"Well, I'm glad everything is going smoothly for you," Mom said. "I remember when Katie and her best friend, Callie, just stopped being friends for no reason. Can you believe that? But, luckily, she made some new friends right away."

I. Could. Not. Believe. It. Mom was telling all my deep, dark secrets to Jeff and Emily.

"First of all, Callie stopped being *my* friend," I said. "And, anyway, why is this important? I have awesome friends now."

"That's exactly what I said," Mom protested.

That's when the waitress came to our table.

Finally, I thought. *We can stop talking about all my horrible school experiences and eat.*

Mom and Jeff both ordered turkey burgers and salads. Emily ordered a turkey club sandwich.

"Would you like fries with that?" the waitress asked.

"I'll have a salad, please," Emily said. "And a glass of water."

Then the waitress turned to me. "What would you like?"

Now, I like to think that ordering food at a restaurant is one of my skills. For example, if we go to Mariani's Italian Restaurant, I always order the eggplant parm, because it's awesome there, but if we go to Torino's, it's too greasy so I get the ravioli, which they make by hand. And I always end up with the best food on the table. It's kind of an art. And whenever I recommend something, people love it. Maybe I'll be a food critic when I get older. Imagine getting to eat in all the best restaurants and get paid for telling people what you did and didn't like. That would be pretty amazing.

Anyway, I know exactly what to order at the Maple Grove Diner. "I'll have the Reuben with cheese fries and a root beer, please," I said.

3

Now, for years Mom and I have eaten out a lot, just the two of us, so she is used to my mad food-ordering skills. But today she raised her eyebrows at me.

"Root beer?" she asked. "You know how I feel about soda. It's so bad for your teeth, not to mention your overall health."

My mom is a dentist, so of course I know how she feels about soda. Which made me think she was just saying that to impress Jeff or something.

"Mom, you know my food-to-beverage formula," I said.

Emily looked interested. "What is that?"

"Well, you know how some things just go together?" I asked. "Like, an ice-cold cola is awesome with Chinese food. But on the other hand, any kind of soda is gross with P-B-and-J. The best drink for that is milk."

"What about . . . a tuna sandwich?" Emily asked.

"Iced tea," I said. "That would go great with a turkey club, too, by the way. Or you can get lemonade."

"Dad, can I get an iced tea?" Emily asked Jeff.

"Well, I'd rather you didn't have caffeine this late," Jeff said. "But I think Katie is on to something. Maybe you can test her theory next time."

"I think it was very mature of you to order

4

water, Emily," Mom said, and I tried my best not to groan out loud. We had hung out with Jeff and Emily kind of a lot over the past few weeks, and Mom was always saying stuff like that. Like she was comparing us, or something.

I was kind of mad at Mom for that comment, so I stayed quiet until the food came. My Reuben smelled amazing—it had corned beef, mustard, melted Swiss cheese, and sauerkraut. I know that might sound gross, but when you eat it all together, it's so good. And the cheese fries were covered with that gooey orange cheese. I ate one of those first.

"Whoops, Katie! You got some cheese on your shirt," Jeff said.

I looked down and saw a glob of orange cheese on my purple shirt. I grabbed a napkin and started scrubbing it, but the cheese just left an orange streak. Mom rolled her eyes and gave a big sigh across the table.

Next to me, Emily was neatly cutting her salad into tiny pieces with a knife and fork. I realized that I had never seen her spill any food or anything like that. In fact, Emily is one of those all-over neat people. Her brown hair is always very neat and shiny, whereas my brown hair usually gets tangles in it by lunchtime every day. She wears white sneakers with no black smudges on them or anything, and I wear sneakers that I've doodled all over with colored pens. There's usually some kind of mudlike substance on them too.

Mom looked at Jeff. "Felix and Oscar," she said, and they both laughed.

"What's that supposed to mean?" I asked.

"It's from an old TV show about two roommates," Mom said. "One was really neat, and the other one was ... messy."

"Let me guess. I'm the messy one?" I said, and Emily giggled next to me.

"It was a really funny show," Jeff said. I think he was trying not to make me feel bad.

"Very funny," Mom agreed, smiling at Jeff, and then they started holding hands at the table.

"Gross!" I mumbled, and then I bit into my Reuben. Mustard squirted out and landed on my jeans. Oh well.

"Oh, I've been meaning to tell you," Jeff said, looking at my mom. "I'm not sure if I can go see that show with you next Saturday. Emily's mom has an unexpected business trip, so Em will be with me all weekend."

Emily's parents are divorced, just like mine. Except I never see my dad, and Emily sees Jeff every other weekend and some days during the week, too. It's hard to keep track of their schedules sometimes.

"Oh, that's a shame," Mom said. Then her eyes lit up. "Hey, it's a matinee, and we won't be back late. Why doesn't Emily hang out with Katie and her friends at their Cupcake Club meeting?"

I almost spit a mouthful of sauerkraut across the room.

"What?" I asked, with my mouth full.

"Well, Katie, you're old enough to babysit now, although this wouldn't exactly be babysitting," Mom said quickly. "And I'm sure you could use some help with your cupcakes."

I was speechless at first. Help? *Help?* At our Cupcake Club meetings, my friends Alexis, Emma, and Mia plan our schedules and go over our budget and come up with new cupcake ideas. We don't need help from anyone, let alone someone younger than we are.

"I would love to help," Emily said a little shyly, and suddenly I felt badly for getting worked up. Yes, Mom thinking Emily was perfect was starting to get annoying, but Emily was pretty cool. And Emma's younger brother, Jake, comes to a lot of our meetings when Emma has to watch him, and Emily is kinda sorta like my younger sister, right?

"Fine," I said.

Mom smiled. "Perfect! Jeff and I can drop you off at Mia's for the meeting and then head into the city. I'll check with Mia's mom to make sure she can drive both of you back to our house."

"I just have to check with everybody first," I said, reaching for my phone.

"No texting during meals," Mom said, and I pulled my hand back and sighed. I had a club meeting tomorrow anyway, so I'd just mention it then.

Emily glanced at her dessert menu and then looked over at me. Her brown eyes sparkled under her perfect bangs. "What's the best dessert to go with a turkey club?" she asked.

I hadn't thought about dessert formulas before. This could get interesting.

"Hmm ... Boston cream pie," I said. "Definitely."

"Dad, can I get Boston cream pie for dessert?" Emily asked.

Jeff laughed. "Sure, why not?"

So Emily got Boston cream pie for dessert, and I got rice pudding, to test if it would go well with a Reuben, which it did. Emily did not spill a drop of chocolate or whipped cream, but I managed to get a glob of pudding on my sneaker. And I didn't care one bit.

8

CHAPTER 2

Something New

$\mathcal{K}$atie, I can't wait to try out that new thing you got," Emma said the next day. "Does it really make two-toned cupcakes?"

I nodded. "It's going to be awesome."

We were in my kitchen, having a Cupcake Club meeting. Alexis was there too. The only member missing was Mia. Her parents are divorced, and she spends every other weekend with her dad in Manhattan. Kind of like Emily, I guess. Anyway, it means that she can't be at every meeting. But all of us miss meetings sometimes, so it's not a big deal.

Alexis was scrolling down the screen of her new tablet. She had found this app that could track sales and expenses and stuff, and she was loving it.

"Katie, if you give me the receipt for that, the club could pay you back," she said. "You're always buying new equipment that we end up using."

I shrugged. "That's what an allowance is for. I love buying this stuff."

"But in order to get a real sense of our profits, we have to keep track of our costs," Alexis argued. "Besides, it's only fair to you."

I wrinkled my nose, thinking. "I'm not sure if I have the receipt. I think I used it to throw out my gum."

"Well, next time, then," Alexis said, going back to her app.

I finished setting up the ingredients for the cupcakes on my kitchen table: flour, sugar, eggs, cocoa powder, vanilla, baking soda, baking powder, milk, and butter.

"So, we need to make two batters," I said. "I thought we could start with vanilla and chocolate."

Then I picked up my latest baking tool: an insert that made two-toned cupcakes. It's a white plastic thing that fits inside the cups in your cupcake pan. For each cup there's a plastic circle with another plastic circle inside. You pour a different flavor or color of batter into each circle, and then take out the insert before you bake them. The finished cupcake will have one color or flavor on the inside, and a different one on the outside.

"So why don't the batters run together when you take out the insert?" Emma wondered.

"I think because cupcake batter is so thick," I said. "Anyway, we'll see. That's what this test is about, right?"

We quickly made the two different batters—we're pretty much pros at making batter by now. Then I put the insert on the pan. It fits only three cups at a time. Alexis carefully poured chocolate batter into the center circle, and then I poured the vanilla batter into the outer circle.

"Here goes nothing," I said, lifting up the insert. Each cup now had a vanilla cupcake with a perfect circle of chocolate in the middle.

Emma clapped. "It works! Cool!"

I rinsed off the insert in the sink. "Let's do the whole pan."

When we finished filling the pan, I put the cupcakes in the oven. While they baked, we made a batch of chocolate frosting.

"Dibs!" I called out, taking the beaters off the hand mixer. Frosting was still stuck to it, and I licked it right off. "Mmm."

Emma laughed. "You remind me of Jake."

"Just Jake?" I asked. "Matt is always grabbing the beaters from me. Sam too."

Emma shook her head. "I guess it's a good thing you don't have three brothers, then."

Emma mentioning Jake reminded me of Emily.

"I have something to ask you guys," I said. "I know we're baking next Saturday, but Mom wants me to watch Emily. Can I bring her to the meeting?"

"Oh, so your mom has another date with Mr. Green?" Alexis asked, wiggling her eyebrows.

I sighed. "It seems like she *always* has a date with Mr. Green lately." I lowered my voice. Mom was somewhere in the house, and I didn't necessarily want her to hear that. "They're going to some Broadway matinee or something."

"Sure, bring her," Alexis said. "She's practically our age, right? It's not like she's some annoying little kid or something. No offense, Emma."

"Believe me, I know how annoying Jake can be," she said.

The timer went off, and I took the cupcake pan out of the oven and put it on a cooling rack. We had to wait until the cupcakes cooled to frost them, or the frosting would just melt everywhere.

Alexis walked over to the pan. "You know, they look just like ordinary cupcakes," she said. "I mean, it's a cool idea, but how would people know they're special? It might not be worth the extra effort to make them."

I pulled a cupcake from the pan with my fingertips. "Let's see if it worked, first," I said. I took a knife and cut right through the cupcake. The chocolate cake center was perfect!

"That is really awesome," Emma said. "I bet people would love these, Alexis."

"Maybe we could cut one open and put it on the display," I suggested. "As an example."

Alexis nodded. "That could work. And our customers are always asking for something new. I'll add these to the order form and the website."

"We should taste them first," I said. (I knew they were going to be great, but I never turn down a chance to taste a cupcake.)

The cupcakes were just about cool enough to frost, so we iced them all. I poured glasses of milk for each of us (cupcakes and milk, the perfect pairing), and then we sat down and ate.

In my first bite, I got vanilla cake, chocolate cake, and chocolate frosting all in one. It was amazing.

"This is soooo good," I said, after washing down the bite with some milk. "Can you imagine all the other flavors we could do?"

"Red velvet and chocolate," Emma suggested.

"Or color combinations," Alexis said. "Pink and purple. Yellow and green. Kids would love that!"

We were quiet for a minute, enjoying our cupcakes and the sweet taste of success. Then Emma's blue eyes lit up.

"Oh, I almost forgot!" she said. "Principal LaCosta stopped me in the hall yesterday. She asked if the Cupcake Club would sell refreshments at the talent show."

"Oh, wow, that would be great," I said. "When is that, anyway?"

"Saturday the twentieth," Alexis said quickly.

"You are like a walking calendar," I said. "Is there anything you don't know?"

"Well, I don't know if this is such a good idea," Alexis said.

"Why not?" I asked.

"Yeah, it's perfect," Emma said. "We always sell a lot of cupcakes at school events."

Alexis started to twirl a strand of her wavy red hair. "I guess I meant that it's not a good day for me. I'm pretty sure I have a conflict."

"Well, that's okay," I said. "Emma and Mia and I could sell the cupcakes. As long as there're three of us, it's usually enough."

"Sure. Right," Alexis said. She was acting a little weird. "Yeah, I'll add it to our schedule."

"Ooh, we could do the two-toned cupcakes in school colors," Emma suggested.

I nodded. "Awesome," I said. "Hey, you know what? We should show Mia."

I cut one of the frosted cupcakes in half and took a picture on my phone. Then I sent it to Mia. She texted me back right away.

Luv it! Save one 4 me!

"So it's official," I said. "We've got a new cupcake in our repertoire."

"Oui! Oui!" Emma said with a giggle, practicing her French.

"Right," Alexis said. She wasn't acting weird anymore. "So, next Saturday we're meeting at Mia's house to make the cupcakes for the flower show. Katie, you're shopping for the ingredients?"

I nodded. "Check."

"And you're bringing Emily," Alexis said, typing it into our schedule.

"Check, again," I said.

I was feeling okay about bringing Emily to the next meeting. It was nice that my friends were cool with it (but of course they would be). And she was really sweet and helpful, and I guess Mom was right—we could always use an extra pair of hands.

But most important, it gave me a new feeling—a big-sistery kind of feeling. I've never had that feeling before, and it felt kind of . . . nice.

Weird, right?

CHAPTER 3

The Only Brown?

$\mathcal{M}$onday morning I was happy to see Mia on the bus. I miss her when she's with her dad.

"How was Manhattan?" I asked.

"Nice," Mia said. "Ava and I went to a sample sale. That's when designers sell the sample clothes they make really cheap. I got this skirt there for ten bucks."

She looked down at her red skirt, which I could tell was shorter in the front and longer in the back. She had on a cute white shirt with it and red flats.

"It's nice," I said. "You look like a candy cane."

"Red and white is a clean and classic combination," Mia informed me. "I read that in a magazine somewhere." She's really into fashion, partly because her mom is a fashion stylist, and Mia always looks like she could be in a magazine. The only way my picture would be in a magazine is if the magazine were called *Messy Cooking* or something.

"How's Ava?" I asked. Ava is Mia's best friend in Manhattan. I used to be a little jealous about that, until I realized that I am her best friend in Maple Grove. Besides, Ava's nice.

"She joined the soccer travel team," Mia said. "She plays, like, all the time. So it was nice to see her. Hey, did you bring me a cupcake?"

I reached into my backpack and took out a cupcake container that perfectly fit one cupcake. "Of course!"

"Did somebody say 'cupcake'?"

George Martinez stuck his head over the back of my seat. George is my friend who's a boy who I like, and I guess *like* like him, sometimes, if you know what I mean. And I'm pretty sure he *like* likes me, too.

"I'm so hungry," George said.

"It's seven thirty in the morning," I said. "Didn't you eat breakfast?"

"Eggs, bacon, oatmeal, toast, and a banana," he replied. "But I'm still hungry."

"Well, I *might* have brought some extras," I said. "But I can't open the box now."

"Aw, please?" George asked.

"Nope," I said.

"Pretty please?" George batted his eyelashes, which made me laugh

"Lunchtime. I promise," I told him.

George shook his head. "You're so mean!" Then he ducked back into his seat.

When I looked over at Mia, she was rolling her eyes.

"What?" I asked in a loud whisper.

"You guys are too sweet," she said. "*You* should be the one dressed like a candy cane."

I think I blushed a little. "We're just goofing around, that's all."

When lunchtime came, George remembered about the cupcake. He brought his friends Ken and Aziz with him.

"Hey, Katie," he said. "So, do you have enough cupcakes for all of us?"

The boys sat down at the extra seats at our table like it was no big deal. Mia made an *I told you so* face at me, and Emma started to giggle. Alexis was busy doing something on her tablet. She looked up, said, "Hey," to the boys, and went back to it. She's been in love with Emma's brother Matt for, like, forever, and doesn't even notice other boys.

"As a matter of fact, I do," I said, taking the container out of my backpack. We make test cupcakes all the time, so I end up bringing them to school a lot. Maybe for George. "Here you go."

I took three cupcakes out of the box and handed them to the boys. Ken and Aziz starting eating theirs right away. But George did something weird.

He leaned his head back and balanced the cupcake on the end of his nose.

"Be careful!" I cried.

"So what do you think?" George asked, still balancing the cupcake.

"I think you're going to drop that cupcake," I replied.

George took the cupcake off his nose and looked at me. "No, I mean about the trick," he said. "I've been practicing balancing different stuff, and I was thinking of doing a balancing act for the talent show."

"A cupcake balancing act?" I asked.

He shook his head. "No, other stuff too."

"It depends on what you're balancing," Mia said. "Can you do, like, a long pole, with plates on top of it, and then spin them around? I saw a guy on the street do that once."

"That's insane!" George said. "I can't do stuff

20

like that. But I can do a broom. And I'm working on a chair."

Emma nodded. "A chair would be pretty impressive."

"Yeah, but you need music or something playing behind you," I said.

"That would be cool," George said, thinking. "I don't know. I just want to do something, you know? Are you guys doing anything?"

"No way!" I said. "I'd be too scared to get up there."

"I don't think I would be scared, at least not after doing my camp talent show," Emma said. "I mean, I could play the flute, but I've already done that."

Alexis didn't say anything; she seemed totally engrossed in whatever was on her tablet screen.

"Besides, we're selling cupcakes that night," Mia pointed out. "That's our real talent."

"You got that right," Ken said. "That cupcake was really good."

"Yeah, George. You should stop balancing yours and eat it," Aziz said.

George unwrapped the cupcake. "I was just gonna do that."

Then Mr. Green walked up to our table—

Mr. Green the math teacher, also known as Jeff, my mom's boyfriend. He doesn't teach any of my classes, but sometimes he has to monitor the cafeteria.

"Hello, Cupcake Club," he said. "I see you're spreading some cupcake happiness today."

George swallowed a bite of cupcake. "I'm definitely happy!"

"Do you want one?" I asked.

"No, thanks, Katie," he said. "I just wanted to thank the Cupcake Club for allowing Emily to hang out with you on Saturday. She's very excited."

"It's no problem," Emma said with a smile.

"Great," he said. "Enjoy the rest of your lunch."

Then he walked away, and George couldn't resist teasing me.

"Your mom's *boyfriend* sure is nice," he said.

I sighed. "Yeah, well, people have boyfriends. It's no big deal."

"Hmm," George said. "I wonder what would happen if they got married. Would your mom become Mrs. Brown-Green? That sounds like a new color in a big crayon box."

He and the other boys started laughing. I probably would have laughed too if George hadn't been talking about my own mom.

"Would you become Katie Brown-Green?"

22

George asked. "That's kind of long. If you got a job at Burger Hut, you'd need a really big name tag."

"Hey, Katie, what do you think of Jason White?" Ken asked me. "He's in our science class. If you married him, you'd been Katie Brown-Green White!"

"Yeah, everyone in Katie's family has to marry someone with a color for their last name," Aziz said. "They'll be known as the Crayons." All the boys started howling at that.

"Very funny," I said in a voice that clearly showed I didn't think they were being funny. Normally, I didn't mind George's teasing, but this was hitting a spot that didn't feel good.

Mia must have seen the look on my face. "If you boys will excuse us, we have some girl business to discuss," she said, looking right at George.

"Ew! Girl business," Ken said. "We're out of here."

"Thanks for the cupcakes," George said, smiling at me, and then the boys went back to their table.

"That was weird," Mia said.

"Tell me about it," I said. "I mean, sometimes I wonder what would happen if Mom married Mr. Green, but I never thought about her changing her name. I guess she would, right? But that doesn't mean I would have to."

"I think that would be up to you," Mia said.

"Right. So you'd still be Katie Brown," Alexis chimed in. "Nothing to worry about. And if your mom wants to be Mrs. Brown-Green, there's nothing wrong with that."

"I guess," I said, but to be honest, something did feel wrong. Let's say Mom *did* marry Mr. Green. She'd be Mrs. Brown-Green. Emily would be Emily Green. And I would be Katie Brown. The only Brown in the family. Plain old brown. Boring brown. Definitely not the most popular crayon in the box. "I don't know," I said. "It's all kind of depressing."

Mia put her arm around me. "Enough about names. Let's talk cupcakes."

That made me feel a little better. But I knew it was going to be hard to get the name thing completely off my mind.

CHAPTER 4

Emily Joins the Cupcake Club

$\mathcal{K}$atie, you have my cell phone number," Mom said, looking back from the passenger seat at me. "Call me if you need anything, okay?"

"Of course," I said. "That's only, like, the seventeenth time you've mentioned it."

It was Saturday morning, and I was sitting with Emily in the backseat of Jeff's car. Jeff and my mom were dropping us off at Mia's house for the Cupcake Club meeting. I don't sit in the backseat of cars a lot; usually it's just me and my mom, and I sit in the passenger seat next to her. Sitting in the backseat was making me feel like a little kid.

Mom ignored my sarcasm. "We should be back by six, before it gets too late," she went on. "Mia's mom is giving you guys lunch, and we'll all get some pizza or something when we get back. If you're hungry when you get home, there are granola bars in the pantry and bananas on the counter. Please don't—"

"Use the oven when you're not there. I know," I said. I don't know why she has to repeat the same rules every single time she goes out. It's like she doesn't trust me or something.

"Well, I am glad you know the rules so well," Mom said just as we pulled up in front of Mia's house.

Mom wasn't the only one giving out parental attitude.

"Emily, I expect you to listen to Katie and the Cupcake Club," Jeff was saying. "And try to be helpful, okay?"

"Yes, Dad," she said, looking at me and rolling her eyes. I smiled. At least I wasn't the only one.

Emily and I got out of the car, and Jeff popped the trunk. We grabbed the bags of ingredients that I had bought that morning.

"Have a good time!" Mom yelled as we walked up to the house.

"You too!" I shouted back.

Mia lives in one of those old-fashioned–looking houses. It's got white wooden shingles and an open front porch. When I rang the bell, Mia's dogs imme-diately started yapping from behind the door.

"That's Tiki and Milkshake, Mia's dogs," I told Emily. "They sound crazy, but don't be nervous, they're pretty tiny."

Mia opened the door. "Yay! You're here!" she said, hugging me. Then she smiled at Emily. "Hi. I'm Mia."

Tiki and Milkshake were jumping up on Emily's ankles. The two dogs have fluffy white fur and black button noses. I can tell them apart because Milkshake always has a pink bow in her hair.

"They're so cute!" Emily said, petting Milkshake's head. "What kind of dogs are they?"

"They're Maltese," Mia answered. "Wow, they really seem to like you."

"They jump up on everybody," I said, and then I felt kind of badly saying it. What was wrong with me? Mia's dogs could like Emily if they wanted to.

"Come on into the kitchen," Mia said, grabbing one of the bags from me. "Alexis and Emma are here."

We followed her into the kitchen, where Alexis and Emma were putting paper holders into four cupcake pans.

"So, this is Emily," I said. "And this is Alexis and Emma."

27

"Hi," Emily said. "Thanks for letting me help today."

Emma smiled at her. "You picked the perfect day to join us. We need lots of help. We've got to make four dozen cupcakes and they're pretty complicated."

"It's going to be so worth it, though," I said. I looked at Emily. "We're making cupcakes for a flower show at the Women's Club tomorrow. So I came up with a really flowery flavor, and Mia knows how to make the best fondant flowers to decorate them with."

"Fondant—that's the stuff that you can roll out, right? It's made of sugar?" Emily asked.

I nodded. "That's the stuff." I had to admit I was a little impressed. "How do you know about fondant?" I asked. I was really curious.

"I watch the food channel a lot," she said. "Especially those cake contests. Those cakes are amazing!"

"Oh my gosh, but have you ever seen when the big cakes fall?" Emma asked. "It's so awful!"

"I know!" Emily squealed. "At first you think it will be funny, but when it happens, you feel so bad for them."

Emily seemed to be fitting in just fine. I started unpacking the ingredients.

28

"So, we've got three things to make," I said. "Vanilla cupcake batter. That's easy. Then the peach filling."

I held up a bag of peaches. "We'll make it from scratch, like we practiced. And then the lavender icing."

I held up a little jar with a thick, pale purple liquid in it. "I finally perfected the lavender syrup. Mom helped me last night. We boiled down sugar and water and dried lavender, and then strained out the leaves. It should be thick enough to flavor the icing without making it too runny."

"Wow, that sounds complicated," Emily remarked.

"It's not, as long as we take it one step at a time," Alexis said, taking charge as she normally does. "Emily, why don't you help me with the batter? Emma and Katie, you guys can work on the peach filling. Mia, why don't you get started rolling out the flowers?"

I saluted. "Yes, sir, general!"

Alexis rolled her eyes and grinned. "You know you'd be lost without me."

I hugged her. "I do! I do!"

Mia cranked some music on her MP3 player, and we started cooking. Making the peach filling isn't so hard; it's just a pain to peel the peaches. After

29

they're peeled, you chop them up and add them to a small pot with water and sugar, and cook it all down until it gets mushy. By the time Alexis and Emily put the cupcakes in the oven, the peaches were the perfect gooey consistency.

Alexis took off her oven mitts and wiped a strand of wavy red hair away from her face.

"Baking makes my hair get so frizzy!" she complained. She glanced over at Emily's sleek shiny hair. "I wish I had hair like yours, Emily. It's gorgeous."

"Thanks," Emily said.

Alexis had a point. Emily's hair is thick and glossy and shiny. Mine isn't wavy or curly like Alexis's, but it's kind of fine, and whenever I'm near a hot oven, it goes limp. But Emily obviously doesn't have that problem.

"So, when the cupcakes come out and cool down, the filling should be cool too," I said. "Then we can inject the filling and frost the cupcakes."

"You and Emma should make the icing," Alexis suggested. "Emily can help Mia with the flowers."

"Oh, Emily, that would be so great!" Mia said, looking up from the kitchen table. "I've got loads to do."

"If you guys don't mind, I want to write copy

for the new flyer," Alexis said. "That way it will be updated for tomorrow."

"Sure thing," I said, and then Emma and I got to work on the icing.

The morning flew by as we worked, and just as the oven timer went off, Mia's mom came into the kitchen. She is superstylish, just like Mia, with perfectly straight black hair. Today she was wearing black pants with ballet flats and a crisp-looking white shirt.

"Are you girls ready for a break yet?" she asked. "I've got sandwiches and a big salad for you in the fridge. We can eat in the dining room."

"This is a great time," Alexis said. "We're waiting for stuff to cool anyway."

"And we can take a break from the flowers," Mia said. "Although there's not much left to do. Emily is amazing at this. Come, look!"

We went over to the table. To make the flowers, Mia and Emily had rolled out fondant in pale purple, pink, yellow, and green. Then they used tiny cutters to cut out flower parts and leaves. Once the shapes were cut, they had to be carefully pressed together and rolled to look like real flowers. I always have a hard time doing it because you need to be really careful and you need to concentrate.

"Look at her roses," Mia said, pointing. "They're perfect!"

I leaned over for a closer look. Emily had taken the pink fondant shapes and rolled them to look like perfect little rosebuds. Then she'd attached two leaves to each one.

"Emily, are you sure you aren't a professional?" Alexis asked.

Emily blushed. "I swear, I've never done this before!"

"I don't believe it," Emma said. "These are too good."

"Hey, we should help Mrs. Valdes get stuff on the table," I said, heading for the fridge.

Pretty soon we were eating lunch around Mia's table with her mom.

"Where are Eddie and Dan?" I asked. Mia's stepdad and stepbrother were usually around.

"Dan has a basketball game this afternoon, and Eddie's watching," Mia's mom answered.

Then Mia's mom had a bunch of questions for Emily. Did she do any after-school activities? What kind of books did she like to read? I could tell she was being extra nice to Emily. And of course there was nothing wrong with that, but it was starting to get to me. It was like everybody was making a big deal about Emily.

Then Emily excused herself to go to the bathroom, and my friends started talking about her.

"Katie, she's really nice," Emma said.

"And talented," Mia added.

"And she's very mature for her age," Alexis said. "I'm impressed. It's not like having an annoying little kid around at all."

"Hey!" Emma protested, knowing that Alexis was referring to Jake.

"Well, she's not," Alexis said.

"Yeah, yeah, I know, she's perfect," I said. "So, Mrs. Valdes, have *you* read any good books lately?"

"As a matter of fact . . . ," she began, and I knew I had succeeded in changing the topic. Mia's mom loves to talk about books.

After lunch, we finished the cupcakes. We used a special injector tool that I have to fill the vanilla cupcakes with the peach filling. Then we iced them with lavender frosting and topped them with the fondant flowers.

"They look like little works of art," Emma said.

Alexis handed one to Emily. "We always make a few extra to test and make sure they came out okay. Could you please do the honors?"

"Sure," Emily said. She carefully peeled the

33

wrapper and bit in, and her eyes got wide. "Oh my gosh, this is the most delicious thing I've ever tasted! You guys are awesome."

"We couldn't have done it without your help," Mia said.

Oh, couldn't we? I wanted to say, but I know that would have sounded mean. I'm just saying—the recipe was totally my idea. But nobody seemed to remember that. This whole "We love Emily" thing was making me kind of grumpy.

"Emily, you can help us anytime you want," Alexis said.

"Thanks, that would be great," she said, beaming.

I guess I should have been happy about this. I mean, I was worried that she would interfere with our baking, right? And the exact opposite happened. So that was great.

Only it didn't feel great. Okay, I'll admit it. I was jealous. Jealous from the top of my limp hair to the bottoms of my dirty sneakers. I could live with the fact that Emily was neater than I was and had nicer hair than I do and whatever. But making cupcakes is my thing. *My* thing.

And maybe it sounds immature, but I didn't want cupcakes to be *her* thing too.

CHAPTER 5

Emily the Perfect

$\mathcal{M}$ia's mom drove Emily and me back to our house around five, so we had about an hour to kill before my mom and her dad came home.

"I'm going up to my room," I said. "I guess you can watch TV or whatever."

"Oh, okay," Emily said. I'm not sure, but maybe she looked a little disappointed that I wasn't going to hang out with her. For a split second I thought maybe I was being rude. But I mean, come on, we spent the whole day together! Was it too much to have an hour to myself?

I was deep into this computer game where you catch flying carrots with bunny rabbits when I heard a commotion downstairs. Mom and Jeff were home.

"Katie, come on down!" Mom called.

I reluctantly quit the bunny game and went downstairs. Jeff was holding two pizza boxes.

"Emily has started to set the table," Mom said. "Why don't you help her?"

I nodded. "Sure." Although, as I went into the kitchen, I was wondering why Mom had sent Emily to do that. I mean, she doesn't even know where the plates are.

Emily had set up four red dinner plates on the table.

"Oh, we don't use those for pizza," I said. It wasn't exactly true—sometimes we did, but they weren't the plates that I liked. I went to the cabinet and picked out four yellow plastic plates. "We use these because they're smaller and they leave more room for the pizza boxes on the table."

"Oh, sure," Emily said. "Sorry."

"No biggie," I told her.

When the table was set, we sat down for pizza. Mom and Jeff told us the whole entire plot of the Broadway show they saw, and Jeff even sang some songs from it. Mom was laughing so hard.

"I'm sure the girls are getting bored," she said. "Save some singing for the barbecue tomorrow."

"What barbecue tomorrow?" I asked.

"Jeff has invited us over for lunch tomorrow at his house," Mom said.

"But I have to set up cupcakes for the flower show," I protested.

"I know, but you'll be done in plenty of time for lunch," she pointed out.

I looked down at my pizza. It wasn't really the flower show that bugged me. It just started to feel like we were seeing Jeff and Emily all the time. And, technically, I see Mr. Green in school every day, so I see even more of him than Mom does!

When Jeff and Emily left, Mom asked if I wanted to watch a movie with her, but I didn't feel like it. I went upstairs and started catching more flying carrots with bunnies. Carrot after carrot after carrot . . . until I got bored and started looking up carrot cake recipes online.

The next morning, Mom drove me to the Women's Club so I could help set up the cupcakes. We pulled up at the same time as Mia and her mom, and we helped them bring in the cupcake carriers. Alexis was already inside, putting a pale-green tablecloth on our table.

"Emma's got an emergency modeling job," she informed us.

I giggled. "A modeling emergency? I need

someone to wear this little black dress, quick!"

Alexis shook her head, laughing. "I think one of the models canceled and she had to fill in. Anyway, this is an easy setup."

Sometimes we have to do fancy displays, but we decided that since the cupcakes were so pretty, they could go on our plain white cupcake towers. As we were carefully setting the cupcakes down on the stands, a woman walked up to Alexis. She wore a pretty yellow flowered dress and had a daisy tucked into her curly brown hair.

"You must be Alexis," she said, shaking her hand. "I'm Rose."

"Nice to meet you," Alexis said. She looked at us. "Rose is the flower show organizer."

I couldn't help giggling again. "You have the perfect name for the job."

She smiled. "I know. I get that all the time," she said. "So, anyway, I set aside some lovely flowers that you girls can add to your table."

"I was thinking we could put them around the base of the towers," Alexis said. "What do you guys think?"

"That would be really pretty," Mia said.

Rose walked off and came back with a basket of flowers. Most of them looked sort of like pom-poms, with lots of rows of petals in pink, white, and yellow.

"Zinnias and pinks," Rose said, handing Alexis the basket. "They'll look great with the colors you've chosen. The cupcakes look beautiful."

We carefully arranged the flowers around the cupcake towers and then stepped back to look.

"Gorgeous!" Mia said.

I snapped a picture with my phone. "This is really nice. And wait until they taste them."

"I'll put some flyers over by the front door, and then I'll tell Rose we're done," Alexis said, heading off.

Mia turned to me. "Do you want to go to the mall? My mom said she'd take us."

I looked at Mom, who had been watching us set up. "Can I?"

Mom sighed. "Katie, you know we have plans. Jeff and Emily are expecting us. Both of us."

I wanted to argue, but I knew it wouldn't do any good. I turned back to Mia.

"Sorry, Mia, but Mom wants me to hang out with *Emily* again," I said.

"You say that like it's a bad thing," Mom said.

Now it was my turn to sigh. "Well, it's kind of like we're seeing them all the time."

Mom looked uncomfortable. "We can talk about this in the car." Then she said good-bye to Mia's mom, and we left.

We didn't talk about it in the car, though. I stuck my headphones into my phone and listened to music. A few minutes later we arrived at Jeff's house.

I have to admit, I was kind of curious to see what kind of house Mr. Green lived in. It was weird, when I thought about it, that he had always come over to our house, but we had never been over there. Well, at least I hadn't. I was sort of disappointed that it wasn't green. It was gray, with white trim and black shutters, and sort of small, like my house. The lawn was very neatly trimmed, and it was big and went all around the house.

"We're back here!" Jeff called out, and we walked around the house to the backyard. It was pretty nice back there, with a big patio and a giant metal grill. Jeff was standing in front of the barbecue, and Emily was setting a round table that had a big umbrella stuck in it.

Mom walked over and kissed Jeff on the lips. Gross!

"Hi, Katie," he said, once their lips were unlocked. "How did the setup go?"

"The table looks great," I said. I took out my phone and showed him the picture. "See?"

"Very professional," Jeff said approvingly. "Well done, Katie!"

"And Emily's decorations looked beautiful," Mom said. "You did a great job, Emily."

"Well, Mia did the decorations too," I reminded my mom. For some reason she kind of glared at me. But Mia actually did most of the decorations. I sighed to myself.

"So the chicken will be done soon," Jeff said. "I've got a green salad inside."

"And I brought the potato salad," Mom said, holding up the bowl. "I just need to pop it in the fridge until we're ready to eat." Then she looked at Emily. "Why don't you show Katie your room while your dad and I get lunch ready?"

"Sure," Emily said.

I followed her into the house. Emily's room was upstairs.

"Um, well, here it is, I guess," she said, kind of shyly.

Her room was small, but it was superneat. Her bed was perfectly made, without a wrinkle in the yellow bedspread. There was a really cute rag rug on the floor, one of those kinds with rainbow colors, which I love. Her dresser was painted yellow, and on top she had a bunch of trophies. And there wasn't an extra scrap of paper or cookie crumb on top of her desk.

"I like your rug," I said.

She smiled. "Me too."

Then there was an awkward silence.

"I don't know why parents always want us to show people our rooms," I said. "Although Mom stopped asking me to do that a few years ago. Mine's always a mess."

Emily laughed. "Lucky!"

I didn't know what she meant by that, and I didn't ask. Then we heard Jeff calling us down to eat.

The chicken was really good, and Emily had made chocolate chip cookies for dessert. Mom made a big fuss over them.

"Emily, you are such a good baker," Mom said. "These cookies are really moist. I can never get mine like these."

What she really meant to say was that *we* could never get ours like these, because Mom and I always make cookies together. So that kind of made me mad. Perfect Emily baked perfect cookies. Of course!

And then, after that, Mom and Jeff were just talking and talking, so Emily and I went inside to watch the cake contest show on the food channel. Then, finally, Mom said it was time to go home.

On the ride to our house, Mom remarked, "Wasn't Emily's room nice? She keeps it so clean. It would be nice if you could keep yours the same way."

That is when I lost it.

"Could you *please* stop talking about how perfect Emily is?" I asked. "I'm getting pretty sick of it. And I'm getting really, really sick of you comparing me to her all the time. All. The. Time! Because we spend all our time with them!"

"Calm down, Katie," Mom said. (I hate it when she says that.) "I never said Emily was perfect. And what's wrong with having a clean room?"

I ignored the question. "You said her cookies were perfect. Her room is perfect. She orders water perfectly. And everyone knows her hair is perfect. Seriously, I'm beginning to wonder if she's human. Are you sure she's not an android that Jeff built in his basement?"

"That is not funny, Katie," Mom said. Her voice was tight.

Then we pulled into our driveway.

"I'm tired," I said when we got into the house. "I'm going upstairs."

Mom didn't say anything. I knew the sun was still shining outside, but I didn't care. I flopped onto my bed.

I obviously was not dealing with this "blended family" thing or whatever was happening with Mom and Jeff and Emily and me. It felt like I didn't fit into that equation. A Brown in a sea of Greens.

That got me thinking. My dad is a Brown. He lives in the next town, and he's been trying to reach out to me. If Mom and Jeff got married, I could always go live with him. If I was with my dad, I'd be a Brown in a family of Browns.

I reached under my bed and pulled out my Secret Shoe Box. It's where I keep stuff that's important. Inside was the news article that the local paper printed about my dad's restaurant. There was a picture of him with his wife and their three little girls—my half-sisters. Weird, right? They were my sisters, and I'd never met them.

Suddenly the idea of living with my dad didn't seem so great. I was doing a lousy job of getting used to Emily. How could I possibly get used to having *three* sisters? No, reaching out to my dad was not the solution to this problem.

I leaned back on the bed and stared at the ceiling.

Things were changing all around me, whether I liked them or not.

And at that moment, I didn't like them one bit. I wanted things to be the way they used to be—just me and my mom. No boyfriends or potential little sisters to have to deal with in my life.

What I really wanted was a time machine.

CHAPTER 6

What's Up with Alexis?

Normally, I was not especially excited to wake up on a Monday morning and go to school, but that morning I was looking forward to seeing my friends and getting a break from the Emily-Jeff thing.

At lunchtime, everyone in the cafeteria was talking about the talent show auditions. They were going to be held every day after school from three to four because so many people wanted to try out.

"It's crazy how many people are auditioning," Mia was saying as we ate our lunch. "I mean, can there possibly be that many people with talent in our school?"

"Well, that's the whole point of the show, right?" Alexis asked. "I mean, probably lots of people have hidden talents and never get to show them off."

"I can pick up socks from the floor of my room with my toes, but I wouldn't do it onstage," I said. "I don't know. Have you ever seen those talent shows on TV? Half of those people think they have great voices and stuff, but then they start singing and they're terrible."

"But the TV producers put them on *because* they're bad," Alexis argued. "That won't happen here. That's why they're having so many auditions, so only the good people will get through."

"It's supercompetitive," Emma agreed. "I would be too afraid to even play my flute now. Did you know that Olivia Allen has been taking private singing lessons to get ready for this?"

"I am not surprised," Mia said. "That girl loves attention."

"Well, not everyone does it to get attention," Alexis said. "Like George. He does it to have fun."

"Are you kidding? He loves attention," I said. "He's a bigger ham than the one my grandma Carole serves on Christmas."

"Well, anyway," Alexis said, "all this fuss about it is good for us, because now Channel Eight is going to cover the show."

"How is that good for us?" I asked.

"Because I contacted their news department and pitched the Cupcake Club as part of their story," Alexis said, getting excited. "They're going to do a feature on us, separate from the whole talent show thing, but they'll film us selling cupcakes that night as footage for the story. They may do the interviews then, too."

I couldn't believe it. I raised my arms and started bowing over the table. "Alexis, you are a certified genius. That is great publicity." And I was pretty excited. Being interviewed for the local news? Totally cool.

Emma was frowning. "But you said you weren't going to be there. We can't do it without you."

"Of course you can," Alexis said. "You're a model, aren't you? So you should be comfortable in front of the camera. If you want, I'll write up a statement for you about how we started the business."

"And then Katie and I can sell cupcakes," Mia said.

"And look fabulous," I added. "But, Alexis, can't you get out of whatever you're doing? It stinks that you won't be there. We're part of a team!"

Alexis's cheeks turned a little pink. "It's a . . . business club thing. I can't get out of it. Sorry."

I looked at Mia, and I knew we were both thinking the same thing: Something was up with Alexis. But before we could ask her about it, she did my latest favorite trick—she changed the subject.

"So, Katie, it was nice having Emily at the Cupcake meeting," Alexis said.

"Well, thanks for letting her come," I said. "The next time my mom asks, I'll tell her no."

"You don't have to do that," Emma said. "Seriously. She's great."

"She's smart, polite, and creative," Alexis said. "It was a pleasure to have her around."

"It makes sense," Mia said. "I mean, Mr. Green is really nice, so of course he would have a nice daughter."

I rolled my eyes. "You guys sound like the Emily fan club."

"Well, it's good that she's nice," Mia said. "Be thankful! You got lucky. Just like I got lucky with Dan as a stepbrother. Mostly."

I didn't like where this conversation was headed. "Hey, nobody said she's going to be my stepsister," I said. "I don't know why everybody keeps thinking that Mom is going to marry Mr. Green."

"Maybe because they spend all their free time together?" Alexis asked.

I didn't have any reply to that. Alexis had a good point. I tried to think of some way to change the subject, but I couldn't. So I took a bite of my sandwich instead. Alexis seemed happy to stop talking too, so we pretty much finished our lunch in silence.

Things were starting to get weird in my life. Not good weird, like videos of cats who sound like humans, but bad weird, like when you don't feel like you know where you fit in in the world anymore.

And the weirdness was about to get even weirder.

CHAPTER 7

All Emily, All the Time

So, since you don't have any Cupcake events this weekend, I planned a special weekend for us with Jeff and Emily," Mom was saying at dinner on Thursday night.

I almost choked on my spaghetti. "All weekend?" I asked. "Besides, it's not true that I don't have any Cupcake things. I promised Emma I would help bake the mini cupcakes for the bridal shop."

Mom frowned. "You really need to tell me these things, Katie. But I understand. That's okay, actually. Most of the things we planned are on Saturday or Sunday. With time worked in for you to do your homework, of course."

"Of course," I grumbled, poking at the food on my plate with my fork. Homework and time with my new sort-of family. What a weekend this was going to be.

"And then she went out to the store and came back with a big calendar, one of those ones you can wipe off," I told Emma the next night as we baked the mini cupcakes. "And she asked me to write all my Cupcake dates there so we wouldn't have any more 'scheduling conflicts.' Can you believe that?"

Emma nodded toward the little mudroom attached to her kitchen—the room where she and her brothers stashed their shoes and backpacks and stuff before they came into the house.

"We have one in there. It's a good idea, actually," she said. "There's so much going on, and this way we can keep track of where everyone is and where everyone needs to be."

"Now you sound like Alexis," I teased. But I was starting to feel like none of my friends under-stood me anymore. I mean, Mom's calendar thing was ridiculous, right? She only had to keep track of me. But I guess now she thought she had to keep track of me, Emily, and Jeff.

I finished pouring the batter into the mini-muffin cups. Every week, we make a big batch of tiny white cupcakes for the bridal shop in town.

They do a small fashion show where models show off the newest wedding dresses, and they serve the cupcakes to their guests. They're small and pretty, and some of the guests have ordered cupcakes from us after that. Emma is the one who always brings the cupcakes there, and sometimes she models bridesmaid dresses too.

"I never get tired of making these," Emma said, sliding the cupcakes tins into the oven. "They're so pretty."

Later on, while we were icing the cupcakes, Emma's brother Matt came into the kitchen. He's a grade above us, and he has blond hair and blue eyes, like Emma.

"Making any extras?" he asked.

"It's the bridal shop order," Emma told him. "So, no."

Matt frowned. "Not even one?"

Emma snapped a kitchen towel in his direction. "None! Get out of here! You eat too many cupcakes, anyway."

"Well, maybe I'll go to Alexis's house and see if she'll bake me some," he said, and then he walked out.

I shook my head. "Actually, she probably would bake him cupcakes," I said. "Unless she's off doing something with the business club." I put down the cupcake I was frosting and stared at Emma. "What's up with Alexis lately, anyway?"

Emma shrugged. "I don't know. I know the business thing is important to her. But it's okay. It's not like she's not working just as hard for the Cupcake Club."

"That's for sure," I agreed. "I guess that's why I wish she was going to be at the talent show with us. She's our rock!"

"Yeah, I'm nervous too," Emma said. "We're still meeting Sunday night to figure out what we're baking for the show, right?"

"Right," I said. "I even wrote it on our new calendar."

It didn't take long to finish the mini cupcakes. Mom picked me up at around nine.

"So, when does our weekend with Jeff and Emily begin?" I asked.

"Tomorrow morning," Mom said. "We're all going for a run together."

That didn't sound too bad. I liked to run, especially if we went around the track in the town park. But the next morning, Mom drove us down to the park by the river.

"What are we doing here?" I asked.

"Emily and Jeff like to run here," Mom said. "I said we'd try it."

"But we have tried it, and we didn't like it," I reminded her. "The river smells all . . . fishy and stuff. And the track is just a boring, straight line."

"We can try something new for a change," Mom said cheerfully, getting out of the car. But her voice was fake cheerful. Maybe someone else wouldn't be able to tell, but I could.

"But this path isn't new to us," I pointed out. "We *did* it. We didn't like it."

"There they are!" Mom said, waving at Jeff and Emily, who were jogging toward us. Then she ran off to join them, ignoring my last comment.

I wasn't about to let them get ahead of me, so I quickly caught up. We jogged all the way down the straight, boring path and then all the way back to the parking lot.

"Wow, that was great!" Jeff said, bending over to catch his breath. "And it's such a beautiful morning."

"You said it," Mom agreed. "We'll meet you at the diner in a half hour, okay?"

"You got it," Jeff said, and then he kissed Mom on the cheek.

"A half hour?" I asked. "I'm starving."

"We should each take a quick shower," Mom said. "We're going to the mall after the diner."

"The mall? For what?" I asked.

"Emily needs some new school clothes, and Jeff asked if we would help pick them out," Mom said. "Her mom's been out of town a lot lately and hasn't had time to take her shopping."

I groaned. I hated clothes shopping. I went with Mia sometimes only because I knew she loved it, and at least Mia was fun to be around.

Mom sighed. "Katie, I really don't appreciate your attitude lately. We have fun things planned today, I promise you. Just relax and go with the flow, okay?"

There is probably nothing more annoying than having someone tell you to "go with the flow" when you're in a bad mood. I didn't talk for the rest of the drive, and when we got home, I quickly showered, dressed, and went downstairs with my hair wet.

"Are you going like that?" Mom asked. She had kept her hair back in a ponytail so it wouldn't get wet.

"It's warm out. It'll dry. Besides, I'm hungry! Let's go."

Of course, when we got to the diner, we saw that Emily's hair was not wet like mine. She had it up in a ponytail like Mom.

"Let's eat!" I yelled, bounding up the stairs.

I started to feel less cranky after I ate a big plate of scrambled eggs, with hash browns and toast, and drank a huge glass of OJ (which is the best drink to go with scrambled eggs, hands down). But my good mood didn't last for too long.

"Let's all take my car to the mall," Jeff suggested. "I'll bring you guys back here tonight."

"Tonight?" I asked.

"After the movie," Mom said.

"*What* movie?" I asked.

Mom and Jeff looked at each other. "We hadn't decided yet."

"We *have* to go see that movie about the kids in sleepaway camp," I said. "Mia said it was so funny, and it won't be in theaters for much longer."

Jeff scrolled through the movie listings on his phone. "I think I know that one," he said, and then he frowned. "Oh, it's PG-13."

"So?" I said.

"Well, Emily isn't old enough for PG-13 movies," he said.

"You know, those ratings are just a suggestion,"

I pointed out. "They'll let her in if you guys are with her."

"It's not that," Jeff said. "It's just that Emily's mom and I have agreed that she can't go see PG-13 movies for another year, at least."

Emily gave me an *I'm sorry* look.

"Okay, then," I said. "What *can* we see?"

Jeff scrolled through his screen again. "Well, there's one about the kittens from outer space."

"Seriously?" I asked. "Do we look five?"

"Katie," Mom scolded.

"Sorry," I said. "It's just . . . that one's kind of babyish."

"What about the one about the baseball team?" Jeff asked.

"Oh, I read about that one," Mom said. "That would be perfect."

"Sure, Dad," Emily said.

I didn't answer, but nobody seemed to care.

"Great!" Jeff said, smiling really hard. "I'll order the tickets right here on my phone. It starts at three, so we'll have plenty of time to go clothes shopping."

"Oh joy," I muttered under my breath. Mom didn't glare at me, so she probably didn't hear me.

So, Jeff drove us to the mall, and we went to, like,

four stores to get clothes for Emily. If Mia had been around, I would have texted her to come with us, but she was at her dad's in Manhattan. I was stuck.

Since we had a late breakfast, we didn't have lunch, but I convinced Mom to get us popcorn at the movies. I couldn't convince her to get candy, though, and I didn't have any of my own money on me, so I was out of luck.

After the movie (which was okay, I guess, but probably not as good as everyone said the camp movie was), I was starving again.

"Can we get Chinese food?" I asked.

Mom looked relieved. "That's exactly what we had planned!" she said. She was probably glad that I wasn't going to complain.

"Sounds good. Golden Palace is right near here," Jeff said.

"So is Panda Gardens," I said. "We always go there."

"But Panda Gardens doesn't have Chicken Amazing," Emily piped up.

"Chicken Amazing?" I asked.

"It's this really good chicken dish with mushrooms and stuff," Emily said. "It's so good, but Panda Gardens doesn't make it."

"But Panda Gardens has the best eggrolls," I

argued. "The ones at Golden Palace are soggy."

"Katie, that was just that one time," Mom said. "Golden Palace is fine."

Then she gave me a look, warning me not to object, so I didn't. We climbed back into Jeff's car and went to Golden Palace. I ordered an eggroll, and shrimp with broccoli.

Jeff reached over the table and put his hand over Mom's hand. "This has been such a great day."

"I agree," Mom said. "It's nice to forget about work and just have a weekend full of fun."

"However, I still have homework," I pointed out. "So it's not exactly a weekend full of fun for me." *And homework isn't the only reason why,* I thought, but I didn't say it.

"Well, we were thinking you and Emily could do homework tomorrow morning, and then we could have a picnic in the park," Jeff said.

There was no escape from this weekend of "fun." But I had one out.

"Mom, as you probably noticed on the calendar, I have a Cupcake meeting tomorrow at five," I said. "It's at our house."

"I know," Mom said. "I thought Emily could stay and help you. Alexis told me how helpful she was last time."

I reminded myself to thank Alexis when I saw her—*not*. And now I was stuck in a bad place. If Mom had asked me privately, I would have told her I needed a break from Emily. But she asked me in front of Emily and Jeff, so I couldn't.

"Okay," I said. "I mean, if you want to, Emily."

"Oh, that sounds like fun. You should try some Chicken Amazing," Emily said, putting a spoonful on my plate.

"Thanks," I said, picking at it. Then I tasted it, and you know what? It was amazing. Like, really amazing.

But I was mad at Mom and feeling cranky again, so I didn't say anything about it.

CHAPTER 8

You Too, Mia?

*Y*ou can probably guess what kind of mood I was in the next day. The morning was okay—it was just me and Mom—but I had a ton of homework to do. Just as I was finishing up, the doorbell rang.

"Who's ready for a picnic?" I heard Jeff say in a cheerful noise. Now, normally, I would have yelled, "Meeeeee!" But I was so over everything. I didn't understand why Mom was forcing this Emily-filled weekend on me.

I shut off my laptop and walked into the living room. Jeff was wearing a green-checkered shirt and carrying a picnic basket, one of those old-fashioned woven kinds. Emily had on a white blouse and blue jeans and brand-new red flats. They looked like they had stepped out of Martha Stewart's magazine or something. *How to Have the Perfect Picnic!*

Then I noticed Mom was wearing this really cute dress: green with blue flowers, and cute blue flats. Mom was never a big dress-wearer, but since she'd started dating Jeff, she wore them a lot. She was a perfect match with Jeff and Emily.

I, on the other hand, was wearing dark-blue plaid lounge pants that you're supposed to wear in the house but that I wear outside sometimes, my summer camp T-shirt, and my nasty sneakers. That old TV show song started going through my head.

One of these things is not like the others. . . .

"Are you ready to go, Katie?" Mom asked.

"Yup," I said in a confident voice that dared her to ask me to change. But she didn't.

"Great!" she said. "Let's go."

Jeff drove us to the park (the one that I like to run in), and we found a spot under a shady tree for our picnic. Jeff even had a red-checkered tablecloth with him. He had made chicken salad sandwiches and deviled eggs, and Mom brought carrot sticks and pickles and a thermos of lemonade.

"And Emily made her famous chocolate chip cookies," Jeff said proudly.

Now, the last time I checked, Emily's cookies weren't exactly famous, but I kept that to myself. I had to admit that the picnic was a pretty good idea. It was a beautiful sunny day, without a cloud in the bright-blue sky.

I didn't really talk much the whole time. I leaned back and looked at the sky. If Mom noticed, she didn't say anything.

When we were done eating, Jeff produced a Frisbee.

"How about it?" he asked.

I couldn't resist. Emily and I jumped up. Jeff helped Mom to her feet.

"I'm not really dressed for this," Mom said.

"Come on, Mom, we're just throwing a Frisbee around," I said.

So the four of us tossed it back and forth, and Jeff started doing these goofy things, like trying to throw it backward or under his leg.

"Hey, I've got one!" I cried, catching it. I spread my arms out wide and started spinning around and around. Then I let go of the disk and sent it flying. "I call this my helicopter move!"

Emily caught it, laughing.

"Come on, Emily, show us your best move!" I called out.

Emily shook her head, still giggling. "I can't!" Then she tossed the Frisbee to my mom.

We played for a while, and then Jeff looked at his watch. "We should get you girls back for your Cupcake meeting," he said.

My good mood evaporated. *You* girls? *Your* meeting? It was my meeting, and Emily was sitting in on it.

"Yeah, we should go," I grumbled, and stomped toward the car.

This time Mom noticed. She ran to catch up with me. "Katie, what is up with you? It's like you flipped a switch and your whole mood changed."

"I'm practically a teenager," I replied. "That's how we're supposed to be, right?"

Mom couldn't argue with that. We piled into Jeff's car, and he drove back to the house. I got the kitchen ready for the Cupcake meeting. We weren't baking, just planning, but the kitchen is the best room in our whole house, and everyone likes to hang out there.

Mia, Alexis, and Emma showed up at the same time, and there was a whole commotion as everyone said hi to Jeff. Then they followed me into the kitchen, and Emily came in too.

"So let's do this," I said, sitting down.

Alexis took out her tablet. "Okay, so we need to plan our talent show cupcakes. We decided to do two-tone, right? In the school colors?"

"That sounds like a great idea."

Everyone looked up at Jeff, who had walked into the kitchen. "Sorry to interrupt your meeting," he said. "But we had some food left over from our picnic, and I was wondering if anyone wanted a snack."

"That would be great," Mia said. "I'm hungry."

He went in the fridge and came out with the leftover sandwiches and carrot sticks, and he put them on the table. Then he put out a plate of Emily's cookies.

"Okay, enjoy," he said before heading back to Mom.

Emma reached for a cookie. "Emily, your dad is so nice," she said, biting into a cookie. "And he makes great cookies!"

"Actually, I made them," Emily said shyly.

Alexis grabbed a cookie and tasted it. "Wow, these are great."

"Thanks," Emily said. It sounded like another meeting of the Emily fan club was starting up, so I tried to steer the conversation back to work.

"So we were talking about the cupcakes?" I asked.

"Right," Alexis said. "So should we do blue

cupcakes with yellow inside, or yellow cupcakes with blue inside?"

"I'm thinking yellow with blue," I said. "We could do lemon cupcakes for the yellow, and the blue could just be vanilla flavored."

Alexis typed that in. "What about the icing? Yellow or blue?"

"We could do yellow and blue, like we did the first time we sold cupcakes at the school fair, remember?" Mia asked.

I would never forget that. We sold our cupcakes and won a prize for earning the most money for the school. It was the whole start of our business.

Emma was frowning. "That's good, but we need something that says 'talent show' too, don't you think?"

"What about stars?" Emily piped up.

Mia perked up. "That's perfect! We could do blue stars on the yellow cupcakes and yellow stars on the blue ones."

"Or you could do double stars," Emily said. She nodded toward the sketchpad and colored pencils that Mia had brought. "Can I borrow those?"

"Sure," Mia said, and she watched as Emily sketched out her idea—a smaller cut-out yellow star on top of a larger cut-out blue star.

"See? Or you could do the yellow one big or the blue one small," Emily said.

"That is perfect!" Mia cried.

I know Mia was just being the nice person that she is. But for some reason, I was starting to feel bad. Jealous, I guess. I was already sharing my mom with Emily, and my Cupcake Club. Did I have to share my best friend, too?

"So, will the stars be cut out of fondant?" Emma asked.

Mia nodded. "Sure, that would be best, I think."

"I think we need to make at least eight dozen," Alexis said, doing some quick math. "We should probably bake the night before. It'll be a lot of work, since we're doing the two-tone. Emily, can you help?"

Wait, what?

"Well, I have to ask my dad," Emily said.

I couldn't believe it.

"So is Emily part of the Cupcake Club now?" I blurted out. "I mean, do we vote on these things or what?"

Everybody just kind of stared at me.

"Well," said Mia, looking around, "Emily is a great helper, and we could sure use the help. Right?" She glanced at me.

68

"Sure," I said, not knowing what else to say. "If her dad says it's okay."

Emily got up. "I'll go, um, ask him." But I could tell she was leaving because she felt uncomfortable.

"What was that about?" Mia asked when Emily had gone.

"Nothing," I said. "It was a normal question, that's all."

"But you sounded so angry," Mia said. "And I think maybe you made Emily feel really bad."

I sighed. "Forget it."

"Seriously, is something bothering you?" Mia pressed.

Normally, I would tell Mia anything. But I was still mad at her. It was like she was taking Emily's side.

"No, I'm fine," I snapped. "Let's just finish the meeting, okay?"

So we finished the meeting, and Emily came back in, and things went back to normal. Well, maybe on the outside they were normal. On the inside, I didn't feel normal at all.

CHAPTER 9

Thank Goodness for Mr. Cheddar!

*A*fter the meeting, Alexis's mom picked up Alexis, Emma, and Mia.

"Emily and I should be getting back home," Jeff said. I was relieved. Finally!

"Katie, we need to talk to you first," Mom said. "Emily's mom is going to be out of the country all next week. She's been going to Haiti to help out the people there."

"Oh, she's a doctor, right?" I said. "That's nice."

"The thing is, I have basketball tryouts after school most of this week," Jeff said.

"So I suggested Emily come here after school," Mom chimed in. "With you. Otherwise she'd have to hang out in the gym for hours, waiting for Jeff."

"Yeah, and it can be pretty sweaty and smelly in there," Jeff said with a laugh.

I let this sink in. "So, Emily would be taking the bus back with me?"

Mom nodded. "Then you two could hang out until I get home, and Jeff will pick up Emily when he's done."

I couldn't believe it. After spending this whole weekend with Emily, I was going to be stuck with her for another week! But what was I supposed to say?

"Sure, whatever," I said.

"Great!" Jeff said. "Emily will meet you by the bus tomorrow. How does that sound, Emily?"

"That's fine," Emily said, but her voice sounded kind of small. She didn't seem thrilled either.

"Then it's settled," Mom said. She gave Jeff a kiss. "I'll check in with you tomorrow. Have a nice night, Emily."

"Thank you," Emily said, and then she and Jeff left.

"Well, that was a lovely weekend, wasn't it?" Mom asked. "I know we're filled up with chicken salad, so I'll make something light for dinner. Maybe I'll just heat up some soup."

"Sure, whatever," I repeated, and then I went

up to my room. No one cared what I thought anymore anyway.

On Monday morning, I was in a pretty bad mood on the bus. Mia was talking to me about something Dan did, but I was barely listening.

Then I heard this squeaky voice.

"Good morning, Katie. Got any cheese?"

I looked up and saw a mouse puppet peering over the back of my chair.

"George! What are you doing?" I asked, looking over the back of the seat.

"It's my new act," he said. "This is my puppet, Mr. Cheddar." He held up the puppet. "How do you save a drowning mouse?" he asked in his squeaky voice.

"I don't know. How?"

"With mouse-to-mouse resuscitation!" the puppet replied, and then George started cracking up.

I was laughing too, not because it was funny, but because George is so ridiculous sometimes. I didn't want to hurt his feelings, but he couldn't use Mr. Cheddar in the talent show. He just couldn't. People would be laughing *at* him, not *with* him.

"You need to go back to your balancing act," I said. "Seriously. This is awful."

"Really?" George asked. "Rats!"

"No rats! No mice! No puppets!" I said. "Or I might be embarassed to be seen with you."

"What? That's not fair!" George cried.

"I'm serious! And didn't you try out already?"

"I did," George said. "But I thought I should jazz up my act. My little brothers love this thing."

"Then save it for them," I said. "Trust me!"

George held up Mr. Cheddar again. "That stinks worse than Limberger cheese!"

I looked at Mia and shook my head, and we both laughed. Leave it to George to get me out of my bad mood.

But all day I kept thinking about how Emily was going to come home with me and how weird that was. At the end of the day, she was waiting by the bus. She looked pretty relieved when she saw me, and for a second I felt bad for not wanting to hang out with her. After all, her mom was off in Haiti, and now she had to take a bus to our house instead of going home. It probably felt weird.

"Hey," I said.

Emily smiled. "Hi."

We got on the bus, and I immediately realized we had a problem: I always sit with Mia.

"Don't worry, I'll find another seat," Mia said,

figuring things out at the same time I did.

I gave her an *I'm sorry* look as she headed for the back of the bus, but Mia just smiled at me. She's so nice. Emily and I sat down on my usual two-seater. George stuck his head over the back of our seats.

"Mia! You shrunk!" he said, looking at Emily.

"Very funny," I said. "George, this is Emily."

"You're Mr. Green's daughter, right?" he asked, and Emily nodded. "He's a pretty cool teacher. Everybody likes him."

"Yeah, thanks. I hear that a lot," Emily said.

And then George just kept talking the whole ride home. I'm not sure why he did it, but I was glad that he did. It saved me from trying to make awkward conversation with Emily.

After the bus dropped us off, we headed into the house.

"George is really funny," Emily said. "Is he your boyfriend?"

I could feel myself blush. "Not exactly," I said. "Kind of. Maybe. I don't know."

Emily didn't press it, which was nice. When we got inside, I went straight to the kitchen, like I always do. There was a note from Mom on the table.

Hi, Katie:

Please make sure that Emily knows she can have a snack. We have fruit and cheese and crackers. Get started on your homework right away. I'll be home at 5:30, and Jeff will be there around the same time to take Emily home.

Love,

Mom

"Are you hungry?" I asked Emily.

"A little," she replied.

I got two plates and put some cheese, crackers, and grapes on each one.

"You can do your homework anywhere," I said. "I'm going upstairs."

"Oh, okay," Emily said.

I picked up my plate and my backpack, went up to my room, and closed my door behind me. I did everything Mom told me to, right?

But, of course, that wasn't enough. . . .

CHAPTER 10

I Lose It

$\mathcal{K}$atie, I don't understand your attitude," Mom was saying.

Jeff had picked up Emily, and they'd left. Mom and I were eating dinner.

I sighed. "What do you mean?"

"When I came home, you were in your room with your door closed, and poor Emily was down here by herself," Mom replied.

"We were both doing homework," I argued. "What am I supposed to do, look over her shoulder while she does it?"

"That's not what I mean." Mom sounded frustrated. "I thought you and Emily were getting along so well. And then all of a sudden your attitude changed. You're not talkative, you hide out in your room, and you're not being especially friendly."

This was one of those conversations where deep down I knew Mom was right, but I didn't want to admit it.

Shouldn't she know why my attitude has changed? I thought. Do I really have to explain it to her?

So I shrugged. "I guess. I don't know."

Mom hates when I do that. "Katie, can't we talk about this? Or are you going to say 'I don't know' every time I ask you something?"

"I don't know," I said. Honestly, the words just slipped out.

Mom put down her fork. I could see she was getting a little teary-eyed. "I just really want things to work out," she said. "I like Jeff so much, and I was so happy to see you and Emily getting along so well. . . ." Her voice trailed off.

Then I felt kind of bad. "Listen, I gave her a snack. I did what you said. What's the big deal?"

"Just promise me you can try to be nice, Katie," Mom said. "You don't have to like Emily. Just be nice, okay?"

"I am being nice!" I protested, my voice getting louder. "Name one mean thing I've done to Emily. One mean thing."

Mom shook her head. "Never mind." Mom

didn't say anything more, but in my head I came up with my own list. Leaving her alone when she was a guest in my house was kind of mean. Saying the Cupcake Club should take a vote on whether she got to help out qualified as mean in my book too. But I didn't say a word.

We didn't talk anymore during dinner, which was awful. That almost never happened to us—at least, not before Mom started dating Jeff. So this whole thing was Jeff's fault, I decided.

But believing that didn't make me feel any better. Not really.

Normally, I would be talking to Mia about stuff like this. But for some reason I hadn't. It was like I had closed off that part of myself. So I was kind of relieved when, the next day at lunch, we had Cupcake business to discuss instead of talking about personal stuff.

"Well, the Channel Eight reporter is all set up for an interview the night of the talent show," Alexis told us. "Her name is Mary Chang. She's going to arrive at six, when you guys are setting up."

"Will we have time to do an interview when we're setting up?" Mia asked.

"Sure," Alexis said confidently. "Also, I checked,

and there have been one hundred tickets sold for the talent show already. So we should probably make ten dozen cupcakes."

I was starting to feel nervous. "Alexis, it's going to be crazy that night. Are you sure you can't be there?"

She nodded. "You know, that business club thing."

"That's weird," Emma said. She had a twinkle in her eyes, like she knew something was up. "Ron DeMillo is in band with me, and he's in business club too, and he said he's going to be in the talent show. So I asked him how he was getting out of the business club thing, but he didn't know anything about it."

"Yeah, that is weird," Alexis said, keeping a straight face.

"Wait, Alexis, are you *lying*?" Mia asked—not in an angry way, but in a curious way. "Because you've been acting really strange about this whole talent show thing."

Alexis turned bright red. "I'm not lying. It is a business club thing—like, a special project I'm doing. You guys will be fine without me."

"You know," Emma said. "I was thinking that we could ask Emily to help us sell that night."

"That's a great idea," Mia agreed. "We could really use the help."

Something snapped inside me. "Seriously?" I said, my voice rising. "You know what? I don't know if I can help at the talent show either. And Emily's so great, you probably won't even realize I'm gone."

Then I got up, left the lunchroom, and walked outside.

CHAPTER II

Alexis's Secret

(O)utside, kids were hanging out at the tables or playing basketball on the court. I felt silly as soon as the fresh air hit my face.

What did I do that for? I asked myself. I wasn't even sure. I just felt so twisted up inside. I wasn't usually a jealous or mean person, but something about this whole Emily situation was bringing out the worst in me. And I usually could tell my friends anything, but I was having a really hard time talking about this with them. Maybe because deep down I knew it was wrong to feel the way I was feeling. And I was ashamed to admit it.

My friends came running after me.

"Katie, are you okay?" Mia asked.

My eyes felt hot, like I was going to cry, but I

tried to hold it in. "It's nothing. No big deal. I'm sorry."

"No, *I'm* sorry," Alexis said. "I don't want you guys to think I'm deserting the Cupcake Club that night. That's not it. It's just . . ." She took a deep breath. "I'm going to be in the talent show!"

"What?" Mia shrieked.

"I knew it!" Emma cried.

I was too stunned to say anything. Alexis in the talent show? This was big news.

"Details!" Mia demanded.

We all sat down at one of the tables. Alexis took another deep breath.

"Well," she said. "Mr. Donnelly from the business club was giving this talk about confidence and how it's an important tool for any business owner. And that's been kind of an issue for me lately."

I nodded. Alexis had gotten really tall recently— it was like it happened overnight. I knew she felt self-conscious about it. She always looked a little uncomfortable when somebody commented on her height. I thought she was gorgeous. I would love to be that tall! Then I could always reach the chocolate chips at the grocery store. They always keep them up high for some reason. And I'd never have to worry about who was standing in front of me during a parade. And I'd be better at some sports—like basketball! I could go on and on with reasons it would be great to be tall, but for some reason, Alexis wasn't feeling that way right then.

"So, anyway, Mr. Donnelly challenged us to do something to build our confidence—to try something we've never tried before," Alexis said. "And so I thought, well, I could audition for the talent show. I didn't even think I'd get in."

"That's so amazing!" Emma said. She looked at Alexis, her eyes shining. "I'm so proud of you!"

Alexis blushed. "I'm really nervous about it. That's why I didn't tell you guys. I'm sorry. I just—it's hard for me to talk about."

"So what are you doing?" I asked. "Dancing? Baton twirling? Oh, I know! You can do that thing where people give you math problems and you solve them superfast—like a human computer."

"I kind of want to keep it a secret if that's okay," Alexis said. "I just—I'm afraid of what you guys will say, and I don't want anything to stop me, you know? I just have to jump in and do it, like jumping into a pool without putting your toes in first."

"Aw, can't you just tell us?" I asked. I hated secrets.

Alexis shook her head. "I promised myself I'd stick to the plan."

I had to laugh. Good old Alexis and her plans.

"Well, can't you at least tell us what you're wearing?" Mia asked.

"I'm not sure yet," Alexis replied. "Dylan said she's going to help me."

Dylan is Alexis's older sister. She's in high school and really popular.

"You'll look gorgeous, no matter what, and I know whatever you do you'll be fantastic," Emma said.

"I hope so," Alexis said. "I mean, you should have seen some of the people who tried out. They're amazing!"

"Did you see Olivia try out?" Mia asked.

Alexis nodded. "Yeah, she was actually pretty good," she replied. "She's got a nice voice."

"Wait!" I cried, feeling like a detective. "That means the people who saw you audition know what you did. So now you have to tell us."

Alexis grinned. "I made sure I was the last one to try out on my day, so nobody saw me. You'll just have to wait and see like everybody else."

"No fair!" I wailed, but I was mostly fooling around. I was pretty excited for Alexis. I would never have had the guts to get up on that stage.

Then she turned to me. "I'd help out if I could, honest. It's just that I need to concentrate on what I'm doing that night."

"Of course," I said. "I wasn't really upset with you, anyway. It's just . . ." I wasn't sure what I wanted to say. "Listen, I'm just in a bad mood lately, that's all. I'm sorry. I don't know why I ran out like that."

"Just don't turn into a drama queen on us," Mia said.

I made a face. "Ugh! Don't even say that. I promise I will *not* become a drama queen."

"You could make a lot of money being a drama queen if you had your own reality show," Alexis pointed out.

Emma giggled. "Imagine if they did a reality TV show about us? *The Cupcake Girls of Maple Grove.*"

"No way!" I laughed. "Can you imagine? We'd have to start fighting and throwing cupcakes and frosting at one another and stuff."

Mia shook her head. "That would be so awful!"

Then the bell rang, which meant we had to get to class. Nobody mentioned my freak-out again, which made me happy. I don't know if they were just being nice or if everybody forgot after Alexis's big announcement.

I will not lose it like that again! I promised myself. But guess what? I broke that promise just a few hours later. Which proves that I was just a total mess! But there was so much going on. It was a lot for anyone to handle, and I hate change and surprises!

CHAPTER 12

George to the Rescue

I was supposed to take Emily back to my house with me after school again. She was waiting out by the bus. Then, as Mia and I were walking to meet her, George ran up to us.

"Wanna come play basketball at the park?" he asked. He nodded to Mia. "Chris is coming."

Chris Howard is who Mia likes and who likes her back. They both bonded when they got braces at the same time, even though Mia's are the clear kind and Chris has a mouthful of metal. But Mia told me she thinks he's just as cute, even with the braces.

Mia turned to me. "We should go," she said. "I just have to text my mom."

I was about to say yes too when I remembered

something. "I have to bring her to my house," I said, nodding over to Emily. "I'm sort of babysitting her."

"Why don't you bring her?" George asked.

Because I don't want Emily in every single part of my life, I wanted to say. *Especially not the part where I hang out in the park with boys.* But of course I didn't say that.

"I don't know," I said. "I'm not sure if I'm allowed."

George turned and yelled to Emily, "Hey, text your dad and see if you can come to the park with us!" Emily looked surprised at first, but then she quickly got out her phone.

George grinned at me. "See how easy that was? Now are you coming or not?"

"Let me see," I said. I quickly texted my mom.

It's okay with me if Jeff says that Emily can go, she texted back.

Then Emily ran up to us. "My dad says it's okay if Katie's mom says it's okay."

"That's what she said!" I told her. "I mean, just reversed. So I guess we can go."

I texted Mom again, and she said she would pick us up at the park on her way home from work.

"We're good," I told George.

"Cool," he said. "Chris is going to grab a basket-ball from his house and then meet us there."

The park where everyone likes to play basket-ball is just a few blocks away from the school, so we walked. Besides me, George, Mia, and Emily, a bunch of kids started walking with us. That usually happened when people decided to go to the park. My friends Lucy and Sophie came with us, and Ken and Aziz, and Eddie Rossi, who's the tallest kid in our grade. He's good at basketball, which I guess is lucky, because everyone somehow expects you to be good at basketball when you're tall.

When we got to the park, Chris was already there, bouncing the ball on the court and shooting hoops. When he saw Mia, he smiled really big. I swore the sun glinted off his braces, almost blind-ing us. I wasn't being mean; those things were just really shiny.

"Okay, let's pick teams," George said, and then my stomach sank. I had been so psyched about going to the park with George and everybody that I forgot actually playing basketball was involved.

Here's the thing: I am just not great at most sports. It's not like I haven't tried. I even went out for the softball team once and made it. I guess I'm not very competitive, and I get really nervous and stuff. So then I started running, which I am good at. I'm pretty fast. And I was happy with that.

But when we played games in gym, it was a problem. I always got picked last for a team. In volleyball, I covered my face with my hands when the ball came toward me. And when we played basketball, I didn't think I'd ever made a basket during a game once. Maybe that was because no one ever passed me the ball. But still . . . it was embarrassing.

While I was worrying about all this, George and Chris picked the teams.

"Okay, so, Katie, you're with me, Emily, Eddie, and Sophie," George said.

I snapped out of my mental vacation. "Aw, Mia's not on our team?"

"Chris picked her first," George said with a wink. He knew Chris and Mia liked each other. I guess everybody in our middle school did.

Then it hit me—did everybody in school know about me and George, too? They had to. But before I could feel weird about that, we started playing.

Here was what I did in the basketball game: I ran around with my hands in front of me in case somebody threw me the ball. It wasn't very effective.

"Katie, cover Mia!" George yelled. Good. I

needed direction. I ran over to Mia and started hovering in front of her with my hands up in the air.

"I feel like a nervous gorilla!" I cried.

But I guess my nervous gorilla thing worked, because when Chris tried to pass the ball to Mia, she couldn't reach past me to get it. George recovered the ball, and then, to my surprise, he passed it to me. I caught it and hugged it to my body.

"Shoot it, Katie!" he yelled.

I was right by the basket, so I guessed he'd figured I had a good shot. I aimed and threw the ball—and it bounced off the rim and back onto the court.

"Nice try!" George called out.

Emily got to the ball first. She aimed, shot, and *swoosh!* Two points.

George ran up and high-fived her. "Good one!"

She just got lucky, I thought. I mean, no way Emily could possibly be good at basketball, too. She was the youngest and shortest one playing. Then again, her dad was the basketball coach. Maybe she just had an unfair advantage.

But then, a few minutes later, Chris tossed a pass to Eddie, and even though he's twice as tall as Emily, she jumped up and caught it before he could. Then she quickly made another shot. This one hit the backboard and went right into the net.

"Go, Emily! You're on fire!" George yelled.

After that, George and Sophie started passing the ball to Emily a lot. I didn't even get a chance to make another basket, but that was probably because I'd stopped trying. I was moping around the court, keeping my arms folded across my chest most of the time. Everyone else was laughing and having fun, but I'd shut off that part of my brain.

All I could think was, *Why does Emily have to be great at basketball, too? And why does George have to think she's so great?*

When the game was over, our team won. George high-fived Emily again. "You should go pro! You are the team MVP!"

Emily looked really happy, but I was feeling the exact opposite. That's when I had my second freak-out of the day—well, sort of. While everyone was talking and laughing, I walked off and sat under a tree by myself.

Maybe I am becoming a drama queen, I thought, but I didn't care. I couldn't control how I was feeling.

George came over and sat down next to me. "Why so sad? We won!"

"Yeah, thanks to Emily," I muttered, poking a twig into the dirt.

"She's pretty awesome," he said. "I guess it's lucky that Mr. Green's daughter didn't turn out to be a jerk, right?"

"It's worse!" I blurted out. "She's perfect! Everyone thinks so. My mom. Everyone in the Cupcake Club. Even you." I felt kind of silly saying that out loud, but it felt good to get it out, too.

"Nobody's perfect," George said.

"Emily is," I said. "She's good at art, which is why Mia likes her. And she's a way better basketball player than I am."

"Everyone's a better basketball player than you are," George teased, and I gave him a light punch in the arm.

"Gee, thanks," I said, moping.

"Do you really think I care about who's a good basketball player?" George asked. "I was being extra nice to her because she's, like, your little sister now or something. That's what you do with your friends' brothers and sisters. Like that day my little brothers came with us to the park. You pushed them on the swings and everything. That was nice."

George was making a lot of sense. I always made sure to be nice to his little twin brothers. (Especially since I accidentally insulted them the first time I met them, but that's another story.) And I was

93

always extra nice to Emma's little brother, Jake, even when he was kind of annoying. I did it because I loved Emma. And he was pretty cute, too.

"That's probably what your friends are doing with Emily," George pointed out. "Maybe even your mom, too. She wants to be nice to Emily because she's in love with Mr. Green. Or should I say . . . *Jeffie!*" He spoke in a high-pitched squeal, imitating, I guessed, what he imagined a girl in love would sound like.

"Ew! They are not in love!" I yelled, but I knew that might be a lie. They were spending an awful lot of time together, and Mom always looked super-happy around him. George paused for a moment, as if he were choosing his next words very carefully. And when he looked at me again, he looked at me shyly, then he looked down.

"And, anyway, you are so awesome in so many ways," he said, looking at the ground. "It would be very hard for Emily to be more awesome than you. In my opinion, anyway."

I knew I was blushing. It was nice to get a compliment from George. Plus, he had given me something to think about.

"Thanks," I said. "I, um . . . You're awesome too. I think that." (Did I sound ridiculous or what?)

George grinned. "Yeah, a lot of people tell me that."

"Except when you do puppets," I teased.

George shook his head sadly. "You do not appreciate Mr. Cheddar."

Then I heard a car horn and looked up—Mom was there.

"See you tomorrow," I said, and then I ran off and said good-bye to everybody else. Emily and I got in the car.

"Did you guys have fun?" Mom asked.

"Yes," Emily answered. "Katie's friends are nice."

"Thanks," I said.

"Your dad is running late, so I thought I'd order us all some Chinese food," Mom said. "I'll order from Panda Gardens."

"You can order from Golden Palace," I told her.

Mom looked at me. "Really?"

"Sure," I said. "Let's get some Chicken Amazing."

I turned around and grinned at Emily in the backseat. Emily smiled back at me, and that made me feel kind of good. I'm not saying that talking to George had magically cured all my bad feelings.

But it was a start.

CHAPTER 13

Finally!

Emily came home with me from school one more day that week. The next time, I stayed downstairs and did my homework with her. Emily actually had a question about one of her math problems for me, and I was able to help her.

You should have seen the smile on my mom's face when she came home.

"It's so nice to see you two girls working together," she gushed, and she was so cheerful that I almost wished I had gone up to my room. I mean, sheesh! Why did she have to make such a big deal about everything?

When Jeff came to pick Emily up, he had some news.

"I'll be able to take Emily home tomorrow," he

said. "And by Friday, her mom will be back."

Emily's face lit up. "Really? When is she flying in?"

"In the morning," Jeff told her. "And she said she'll pick you up from school. She's missed you."

"I miss her, too," Emily said.

Until then, it hadn't even occurred to me that Emily might be feeling sad about being away from her mom. I didn't know what that was like. My dad was never part of my life, so I didn't have to shuttle back and forth between two parents, like Emily and Mia did. Mia said you get used to it, but still, it had to be hard, right?

Then Emily turned to me. "Thanks for your help, Katie," she said, and I could see that Mom was totally beaming at Jeff, like *Look! Isn't that sweet?* Once again, sheesh!

And even though I was getting over the whole being jealous of Emily thing, I was relieved her mom was back. For one thing, that meant she wouldn't be at our Friday night baking session.

It was going to be a mammoth one, because we had to bake ten dozen cupcakes for the talent show on Saturday night. Alexis said we could bake at her house, since her kitchen has a big island in it that gives us lots of room for making batter and filling up pans. We needed to get an early start, so we were all going to Alexis's house after school.

Mom and I had shopped for the ingredients the night before and then dropped them off, along with extra cupcake tins and two-toned cupcake inserts. We also needed two dozen eggs, extra flour, butter, and sugar, and we were out of vanilla again. Mia took care of getting the fondant and the tiny star-shaped cutters.

"So I've worked out a strategy," Alexis said, once we were gathered in her kitchen. "Let's all start on batter and filling the baking cups. Once everything's in the oven or ready to go into the oven, Katie and I can do icing while Emma and Mia cut out the stars. Sound good?"

"How about Mia and I do the lemon batter and you guys do the vanilla batter?" I asked.

"Sounds like a plan," Emma said. "I brought over my stand mixer so we can whip up two batters at once."

Emma has this amazing pink stand mixer that she saved up for. It's very cool. If they still made one in purple, I would probably buy the same one.

So we got to work, cracking eggs and measuring flour and squeezing lemons. Alexis said, "It's too bad Emily's not here with us. We could use some extra hands tonight."

You might be thinking that I freaked out again when she said this. Well, I almost did. And I saw Mia look at me like *Uh-oh*. But I remembered what George had said, and I stayed calm. In fact, I did something that I should have done before—I talked to my friends about how I was feeling.

"Um, listen," I said. "You guys could probably tell, but this whole Emily thing is kind of weirding me out."

Mia nodded. "I thought so, but you weren't saying anything, so I wasn't sure."

"It's just—" I put down the measuring spoons I was holding. "I like Emily. She's nice. There's nothing wrong with her. But it's, like, now she's in every single part of my life. I'm just not used to it."

Alexis nodded. "I can understand that. I mean, Dylan's been my older sister my whole life, so I'm used to her. But if she suddenly showed up now and started bossing me around and criticizing my clothing, I'd be like, who is this?"

"Exactly!" I said. "And, Mia, I know you had to get used to Dan, but I mean, it's not like he hangs out with us or comes to Cupcake meetings. But Emily—it's like everybody expects me to do everything with her. Especially my mom. If Emily was really my sister, I'd have had ten years to get used to her being around. It's like my mom wants me to feel like I've known her for ten years in only one week. And she's always around. Like, always."

"Your mom is probably being extra nice to Emily because she likes Mr. Green," Emma said.

"That's what George said!" I practically yelled. "And then—well, I was kind of jealous of the way you guys liked her so much."

"Oh my gosh, are you serious?" Mia asked. She spun around to stare me, and she twirled so fast, she forgot that in one hand she was holding the open flour container, and a cloud of flour filled the air.

I laughed. "Yes, I'm serious. She's so good at art and everything, just like you."

"So you thought I liked her better than you?" Mia asked. "Katie, duh! You're my best friend!"

I was kind of embarrassed about how silly I felt. I mean, Mia was right. We were best friends. Why had I even worried that Emily would come between us?

"And by the way, Emily is probably not perfect," said Mia. "Look, I kind of know what you're going through. There are things about Dan that drive me crazy, as you know. Like how he loves to blare heavy metal music in his room—usually when I'm trying to study. But all in all, he's a pretty great brother. And the same goes for Emily. Just think of what she might have been like. She could have been mean, she could have been nasty. She could have been like Olivia Allen!"

I shuddered, suddenly realizing how lucky I was and how awful my life could have been.

"Well, I was just being extra nice to Emily because she's Mr. Green's daughter, and she's, like, connected to you now," Alexis said. "I would always be nice to someone who you were friends with or related to. Not that you are related yet or anything."

I nodded. "Yeah, I finally figured that out. But it shouldn't even matter why you're being nice to her. I mean, you guys can be nice to whoever you want."

"But if you don't want Emily to come to any more Cupcake meetings, we understand," Emma said. "Trust me. I love my brothers, but I like having time away from them. So I get how you feel. We won't invite her anymore."

I thought about that. "I'm not sure she can't come to any meetings," I said. "I mean, she is really good at decorating and stuff. But I don't think I want her here all the time, you know? Maybe just once in a while."

"What about tomorrow night?" Mia asked. "We really could use some help selling cupcakes. I have a feeling it's going to get crazy."

I nodded. "That makes sense. I'll text her."

I wiped my hands on a towel and texted Emily.

Can u help us sell cupcakes 2morrow night at the show?

She texted me back right away.

I just asked my mom and she said yes! Thanks!

I looked at Alexis. "Do we have any extra Cupcake T-shirts?" I asked. Mia had designed a logo for us that said THE CUPCAKE CLUB, and we had them put on T-shirts. They were really cute, and we wore them to different events.

Alexis nodded. "It was cheaper to order a large quantity, so I have extras."

"Can Emily have one?" I asked.

"Of course," she said. "Everyone who sells cupcakes should wear one. And we should also discuss giving Emily a portion of our profits tomorrow."

Whenever we do an event, some of the money goes into a fund to buy supplies, some of it goes into savings, and the rest of it gets divided between the four of us.

"It shouldn't be a full share since she's not baking," Alexis said. "How about I give her half of my share, since I'm not selling?"

"That sounds good to me," I said, and Emma and Mia nodded in agreement.

I quickly texted Emily.

You will get a T-shirt and we will pay you too.

And she texted back: ☺

"She really is pretty nice," I said. "I guess if I am going to have a little sister, she's not so bad. I just don't know if I'll ever get used to things. I mean, it's always just been me and my mom. Everything's different. It's like I'm starting my whole life from scratch."

"Well, you know, stuff that's made from scratch is much better than stuff that comes from a box," Alexis pointed out. "That's why we don't make cupcakes from a mix."

"Speaking of cupcakes, we'd better get baking," I said, stifling a yawn. "I know it's early now, but I don't want to be up all night doing this."

It didn't end up taking us all night, but it did

take a long time, especially since we were doing the two-toned cupcakes. We had to pour one batter into the mold at a time, move the mold again, and pour again. Then we had to mix up more batter. We had a real assembly line going. By the time we had the last cupcake pan in the oven, we had been baking for three hours.

"You girls need a break," insisted Mrs. Becker, Alexis's mom. She's very organized and focused, just like Alexis. "I have set up some sandwiches and salad for you in the dining room. Please have something to eat before you fall asleep in that batter."

So we took a quick break to eat, and then Alexis and I got to work on the two batches of icing—yellow and blue—while Mia and Emma rolled out the fondant and cut out the stars. We all worked together to put the stars on the way Emily had suggested. They looked so good that I took a photo of them and sent it to her. I got three more ☺s back and a lot of exclamation points.

When the cupcakes were done, we carefully packed them into our carriers and extra boxes, because we didn't have enough carriers for all the cupcakes.

"We should probably invest in more carriers," Alexis said, making a note on her tablet.

"Hey, we haven't done a test one," Emma realized.

"Let me get my dad," Alexis suggested.

Mr. Becker was yawning when Alexis brought him in. She handed him a cupcake covered with yellow frosting and decorated with yellow and blue stars. He immediately woke up.

"School colors," he said. "Nice."

Then he bit into it. He looked at the inside of the cupcake, and his eyes got wide.

"What do you know? Two different colors? How did you do that?" he asked. "That's pretty cool."

"It's a trade secret," Alexis told him.

"Well, I'm impressed," he said. "Tastes good too. The lemon is very refreshing."

"Refreshing," Alexis repeated, typing into her tablet. (She took notes on just about everything, but they came in handy. If a client ever wanted us to describe our lemon cupcakes, we'd have been able to have said that they were "refreshing.")

We were all pretty tired by the time we cleaned up.

"So, um, can one of you guys bring the cupcakes in tomorrow?" Alexis asked. "I'll be, um, kind of busy before the show."

"I almost forgot!" I said. "I am so dying to know what you are going to do tomorrow."

"You'll find out soon," Alexis said with a grin.

"Fine." I sighed. "I'll ask my mom if we can pick them up."

"Maybe you can get me on the way, and I'll help carry," Mia suggested.

"And I could meet you here," Emma said.

I smiled at my friends. "You guys are the most awesome friends ever, you know that? I'm sorry if I acted like a jerk the other day."

Mia hugged me. "Act like a jerk all you want. We will still love you."

That night, I went to bed excited for the next day. It was the first time I had felt that way in a long time. It was a good feeling, and it was all thanks to my friends.

CHAPTER 14

Lunch. School. Cupcake.

*W*hen Mia and I got to Alexis's house the next day, her dad answered the door.

"Hey, girls," he said. "The cupcake containers are inside."

Emma ran up behind us. She lives a few houses away from Alexis.

"Can we see her?" Emma asked.

"As a matter of fact, I am under strict orders *not* to let you see her," Mr. Becker replied with a twinkle in his eyes. "I believe she wants to keep everything a surprise."

Emma walked to the bottom of the stairs. "Alexis, you have to at least show us what you're wearing!" she called up.

Alexis's big sister, Dylan, responded. "Alexis

can't talk right now. And her outfit is a surprise."

I looked at Mia. "Is she wearing a chicken suit or something?"

Mia giggled. "Can you imagine?"

Emma looked at us. "I am going to go crazy! She has never kept a secret from me for this long before."

"Do you girls need help carrying the cupcake carriers?" Mr. Becker interrupted. "I know Alexis wouldn't want you to be late."

"Sure, thanks," I said, and we carried all the cupcakes out to my mom's car and stacked them neatly in the hatch. She had one of those trunk organizers, so the carriers wouldn't slide around when the car moved.

When we pulled up to the school, Jeff and Emily were waiting for us by the front entrance. Emily was wearing her Cupcake Club T-shirt. Jeff had stopped by our house earlier that morning to pick it up.

"Hi!" she said. "Thanks for the shirt. It's really nice."

Emma smiled at her. "Every official helper gets a shirt."

"Gee, can't I get a shirt?" Jeff asked.

Emily rolled her eyes. "Dad, tasting doesn't count as helping!" she complained.

"Maybe if you help us carry in these cupcakes," I said. "Although I'm not sure if we have a shirt in your size."

Jeff laughed. "No problem. I'll carry cupcakes for you guys whenever you want."

We carefully brought the carriers inside and set them down next to the folding table that had been set up for us right outside the entrance to the auditorium. Mia covered the table with a tablecloth she had made: blue with cut-out yellow stars glued to it.

"Ooh, that's so pretty!" Emma said.

Mia grinned. "And that's not all." She opened up a box she had brought from the car. Inside were our cupcake display stands. We'd used some of our first profits to buy the stands. They were big, round plates set on top of posts. The posts were different heights, which made the display look more interesting.

The basic stands were white plastic. Mia figured out that we could customize them for different events by making little tablecloths and draping them over each post. She got big paper or plastic tablecloths and then cut them into smaller circles to fit over the stands. For the talent show, she'd made blue covers with yellow stars, and yellow covers with blue stars to match the cupcakes.

109

We helped Mia set up the stands, and then it was time to start placing the cupcakes. I was opening the first carrier when a woman in a red skirt and blazer walked up to us. Behind her was another woman with a big camera—the kind they use to record news events.

"You must be the Cupcake Club," the woman said. "I'm Mary Chang."

She had a perky voice and perfect, white teeth. Not one hair on her head was out of place. Even if she didn't have the camerawoman behind her, I would have guessed that she was a news reporter.

I felt nervous right away, but thankfully, Emma spoke up.

"Hi," she said. "I'm Emma Taylor. Alexis told me to expect you."

"Well, then we want to do a short feature on you girls," she said. She nodded to the camerawoman. "Alexis filled us in on all the details, so Shannon here will film you while you're setting up. Then I'll ask you a few questions, if that's okay."

Emma nodded. "That would be great. Thanks!"

So we started to put the cupcakes on the stands, but it was kind of weird with this big camera lens following us around and bright lights shining on us. I kept trying not to look at the camera, but I knew

I kept staring at it. It was really weird, and then all of the sudden I was self-conscious.

"Just be natural," Mary Chang called out, and I had a feeling she was talking to me.

Finally, we had the stands covered with cupcakes. The extra cupcakes were still stashed safely in their carriers.

"Okay, great," Mary said. "So, why don't you girls stand behind the table so we can see you and the cupcakes together, and I'll ask you some questions, okay?"

"Sounds good," Mia replied. Like Emma, she sounded really confident. But my palms were starting to get all sweaty, which is not a good thing when you're selling cupcakes.

"So, how did you girls get the idea for the Cupcake Club?" Mary asked.

"It started on our first day of middle school, when Katie brought a cupcake to lunch," Emma said, pointing to me.

"Um, right," I said. "Lunch. School. Cupcake." I had no idea what I was saying!

Mary put the microphone in front of Emily's face. "Aren't you adorable? So, tell me, how do you come up with your cupcake flavors?"

"Oh, I'm just a helper," Emily replied. "Katie is

a total baking genius. You should talk to her."

I was flattered Emily said that, but I was panicked, too. *Flavors? What are flavors?* It's like my mind went blank.

Luckily, Mia knows me really well. She saw the panicked expression on my face and jumped in.

"We all come up with flavor ideas," Mia said. "And then we test them before we make them for real."

I gave Mia a grateful look. The reporter talked to mostly Mia and Emma after that, and I was glad when it was all over and Mary put down the microphone.

"That was great," Mary said. "I'll e-mail Alexis and let her know when it's going to air."

"Thanks," Emily said.

Mary turned to her camerawoman. "Let's figure out the best way to shoot this talent show," she said, and the two of them went into the auditorium.

"I can't believe I was so nervous!" I cried, shaking my head. "'Lunch. School. Cupcake.'? What was wrong with me? You guys were great."

Emma laughed. "Don't worry. They'll probably edit most of it out, anyway," she said.

I sighed. "I hope so."

Then people started coming in to take their

seats for the talent show. Emma picked up the cash box that Alexis had prepared for us. It held lots of fives and singles for change.

"Here we go," Mia said with a grin.

It got busy right away. Our colorful stand got a lot of attention, and people walked right up to it. Mia and Emma took orders and money, and Emily and I handed people their cupcakes. The best part was when people bit into them and then saw the two different colors.

"This is so clever!" one woman said. "I'd love to get some like these for my sister's baby shower next month. Do you girls do parties?"

"Of course we do," I said, channeling my inner Alexis. I handed her a flyer. "You can contact us by phone or through our website."

After about a half hour of chaos, things got quiet, and it came time for the show to begin.

"I just thought of something," I said. "If we have to watch the table, we'll miss the show! We won't see Alexis!"

"Well, there won't be much business while the show is on," Mia reasoned. "So we can watch the show through the doors."

"Perfect!" I said, and we all huddled by one of the doors to watch.

Principal LaCosta walked up to the microphone onstage.

"I'd like to welcome all of you to the Park Street Middle School Talent Show," she said. "There are some wonderful acts in store, and these students have worked very hard. So make sure you give all of them lots of applause."

Everyone clapped like crazy, and then the curtains parted. Music started playing over the speakers—the kind of music you'd hear at a circus—and then George came onstage. He was wearing a tuxedo. Seriously—a tuxedo! Behind him was a table with a bunch of stuff on it. There was a chair behind it.

I was expecting George to say something, but he didn't say anything. Instead, he picked up a feather duster from the table. He tilted his head back, put the handle part on his nose, and then let go.

I started to giggle, and some people clapped. Balancing the feather duster was pretty cool. But that was just the beginning. Next he balanced a really tall broom on his nose! That got a lot of applause. Third he did a little wooden chair. That looked really hard. And then he balanced a Wiffle ball bat, and he picked up three oranges and started to juggle them. He didn't drop the oranges or the bat.

George ended by letting the oranges fall to the ground and catching the bat in his hand. He gave a bow, and everyone clapped and cheered.

"He is, like, the perfect boyfriend for you," Mia whispered to me, and I knew I blushed. But she had a point. I mean, I could really appreciate a talent like that.

Next up was Olivia Allen. She was wearing a sparkly, short, silver dress and silver heels. She sang along to a recording of a popular song, and I had to admit she sounded pretty good for most of it. It was one of those songs where the singer really belts it out. Olivia had trouble hitting some of the notes at the end, but she got a lot of applause, anyway.

Then two girls came out and did this dance with scarves, and this boy did a pretty cool tap dance. Next, Wes Kinney came out and started telling jokes. I thought they were pretty lame, but his friends were all laughing really hard and yelling out stuff.

Then a boy came out carrying a stool and a guitar. He sat down on the stool and started to strum. He looked like a high school boy, and I was wondering what he was doing in a middle school talent show.

But he wasn't the act. A tall, beautiful redhead

wearing a simple black dress walked onstage, holding a microphone. It took me a few seconds to realize who it was.

It was *Alexis*! Mia grabbed my arm real tight, and we tried hard not to scream. Alexis looked amazing!

And then she began to sing. . . .

CHAPTER 15

What a Night!

𝒾 had to stop myself from screaming and cheering because I wanted to hear Alexis sing. The whole audience got quiet; Alexis had this really sweet, pretty voice. I was shocked. I had never heard Alexis sing before. Okay, maybe I'd heard her sing "Happy Birthday" or I'd heard her sing when we played the radio in the car, but not really sing by herself. I didn't even know she *liked* to sing!

The song sounded familiar, but it wasn't one of those popular, belt-it-out-loud songs like the one Olivia sang. It was soft and pretty and had a nice melody.

"She's so good!" Emma whispered to me, and I nodded in agreement.

The crowd thought so too, because when Alexis

finished, she got more applause than anybody else had gotten, I swore. She blushed a little, took a bow, and then left the stage.

Emma, Mia, Emily, and I ran back to the cupcake table.

"Oh my gosh!" I whispered loudly. (The auditorium doors were still open.) "I can't believe it!"

"She is such a good singer," Emily said.

"I have got to talk to her," Emma said. "Do you guys mind watching the table while I go backstage?"

"Go!" Mia said, giving her a push.

A few minutes later people started coming out of the auditorium—it was intermission. We were busy selling cupcakes when Emma came up with Alexis.

"Sorry, I'm late!" Emma said, sliding behind the table. "It took forever to get to Alexis. She was surrounded by hordes of admirers."

Alexis laughed. "Yeah, right." She looked down at her dress. "Sorry, I can't help, but if I get frosting on this, Dylan will kill me."

Up close, I could see what a fabulous dress it was. The black dress came just to her knees and had short sleeves and a sparkly band around the waist. She had on shoes with heels that weren't superhigh but that still made her look even taller. She wore glittery earrings, and her beautiful red hair was blown out straight and shiny and styled like a supermodel's.

"You are way too glamorous to be selling cup-cakes," I said. "But don't worry. We've got Emily helping us, so we'll be fine."

Emily smiled at me, and then I looked up at the customers and saw Mom and Jeff standing there with giant goofy grins on their faces. I knew that they had just heard me and were thrilled that Emily and I were getting along. A few days before, I would have been annoyed, but I just smiled back. It didn't seem like such a big deal anymore.

When intermission was over, we still had some cupcakes left—about a dozen.

"I know," Alexis said. "Let's bring them back-stage and see who wants one."

We followed Alexis "backstage," which was the school cafeteria, where everybody was either get-ting ready to go onstage or relaxing after being onstage. George ran up as soon as he saw us.

"Nice tux," I said. "And I liked your act. Pretty impressive."

"Was I good enough for a cupcake?" he asked, eyeing the box in my hands.

"Of course," I said, handing him one. "Just don't try to juggle it."

It was fun walking around, giving out cupcakes. Olivia was talking to the two scarf dancers.

"I could feel every eye in the audience on me," she was saying. "They were hanging on my every word. It was so unnerving!"

"You were good," I told her.

"Oh. Thanks," Olivia said with a toss of her thick, brown hair. I could tell she was trying to act as if she got millions of compliments every day, but I knew she was secretly thrilled.

"Want a cupcake?" I asked.

"Oh yes! All that singing made me absolutely *famished*!" Then she grabbed one out of the box.

As we walked away, I said to Mia, "Now *that's* a real drama queen. You don't have to worry about me."

"I know I don't!" Mia said.

Since all the cupcakes were gone, we got to go inside and watch the show. We found a few seats in the last row. It was a lot of fun, and when it was done, we caught up with Mom, Jeff, and Alexis's parents outside.

"We'd like to take everyone out for ice cream," Mr. Becker said, "to celebrate your fantastic cupcake sales—and Alexis's big debut. Wasn't she just amazing?"

"Thanks, Dad!" Alexis said, hugging him.

"I got it all on video," he said. "One day, when you're a big star, you can sell the footage for big bucks."

Alexis laughed. "I do not want to be a big star. I just did that to see if I could. Now I can cross it off my list."

"No way! You have to keep singing," Emma insisted.

"Maybe you can convince her over ice cream," Alexis's mom said.

We split up and got into our cars to head to Fletcher's, an old-fashioned–style ice-cream parlor. The chairs are black metal with red-and-white-striped cushions, and the people who sell the ice cream wear red-and-white–striped shirts, big white aprons, and those little hats that look like folded triangles. We found a table big enough for all of us, and the parents sat at one end. I was all the way at the other end, between Mia and Emily.

We placed our ice-cream orders (I got a black-and-white ice-cream soda, which means it's vanilla ice cream with chocolate soda), and then everybody started fussing over Alexis.

"Seriously, Alexis, why don't you at least join chorus or something?" I asked her. "You have such a nice voice."

"I might," Alexis admitted. "If I can fit it into my schedule."

Dylan was sitting across from us.

"Dylan, you did a great job styling her," Mia said. "If my mom ever needs an assistant, I will tell her she should hire you."

Dylan looked really flattered. "Wow, thanks. But Alexis is easy to style."

"Because I let you do whatever you want to me?" Alexis asked.

"No, dork, because you're beautiful," Dylan said.

"I think that's the nicest thing you've ever said to me," Alexis said. "Including the dork part."

I knew Alexis wasn't kidding. Dylan could be really mean to Alexis when she wanted to. Or she just acted like Alexis was the biggest pain in the world—kind of like I had been acting toward Emily.

I turned to Emily. This wasn't going to be easy, but I wanted to say it.

"So . . . I've been meaning to apologize to you," I told her. "I'm sorry if I was acting mean to you lately. It's just . . . I don't know. I guess I was jealous.

My mom thinks you're so perfect and, well, you kind of are."

Emily looked surprised. "Seriously? You think that?" she asked. "Because I am *so* not perfect."

"Yes, you are!" I argued. "Your hair is always shiny and perfect. Your room is superclean. And you don't make a mess when you eat."

"Well, maybe that last part is true," Emily admitted. "But the other stuff is hard. I mean, I have to wake up extra early to blow-dry my hair every day. And my room is so clean because my dad makes me clean it, like, every time I'm there. He's like a drill sergeant."

I looked down the table at Jeff, who was talking and laughing with my mom. Everyone said he was such a laid-back teacher. I had a hard time thinking of him being so strict.

But once I thought about it, it made sense. He was always telling Emily to retie her shoes and put her napkin on her lap when we went out to eat.

"I never thought of it like that," I said.

Emily nodded. "I was always jealous of *you*," she said. "Your mom doesn't give you a hard time about your room. And you have awesome friends and they all love you. And you never stress out about your hair and stuff, but you always look really cute."

I couldn't believe Emily was saying all this. "Really?" I asked.

"Yeah," she said, and then she looked down at her hot fudge sundae with extra cherries. "You know, I was nervous that you wouldn't like me."

I honestly had never thought of that, either. "Well, I hope you're not worried anymore, because I definitely like you."

Emily looked relieved, and then the two of us started laughing. "It's funny how we were both feeling the same way," I said. "I feel silly now."

"Well, you are silly," said Mia, who had just joined our conversation.

When we were done with our ice cream, there were lots of hugs all around.

"Good-bye, superstar!" I called to Alexis as we left the ice-cream parlor.

"I am not a superstar!" she protested, but then just at that moment, a boy walked past her and stopped.

"Hey, you were in the talent show tonight. You were great," he said.

"Thanks," Alexis replied, and I was laughing so hard.

"See? You can't even get ice cream without being recognized!" I yelled.

I was still laughing when Emily and I got into the backseat of Mom's car. The plan was to drop her and Jeff back at school, where Jeff's car was parked.

Mom turned on the radio, and the rock station I'd been listening to came on. Mom looked into the rearview mirror.

"What's that station you like again, Emily?" she asked.

"Ninety-four point one, but you don't have to change it," she said, giving me a nervous look, but I gave her a look back to show that I was okay with it.

"No, it's my pleasure," Mom said. "That's the one I like too." It was not the one I liked, but it was fine.

I leaned back in my seat. *I guess this is how life is going to be from now on,* I thought. *Filled with compromises.*

Alexis and Emma complained about this kind of thing all the time, and even Mia complained about Dan. I had never understood it before. I guess I was in kind of a bubble, being an only child. I'd never even had to share my mom with anyone.

And it looked like Jeff and Emily weren't going anywhere anytime soon. There was a good chance that this change was going to be permanent. So I was definitely starting from scratch.

I remembered what Alexis said about baking from scratch—about how we do it because our cupcakes taste so much better that way. Whatever this new life held, I guessed we were starting from scratch too. And while I knew it wouldn't be totally smooth, I had a feeling it might just be as sweet as the icing on one of our cupcakes.

CHAPTER 16

Cupcake Club Celebrities!

I had worked things out with my friends. I had even worked things out with Emily. But there was one person left I needed to talk to: my mom. So I was glad when we dropped Jeff and Emily off and headed home. I didn't even have to bring up the topic, because Mom gave me the perfect opening.

"So, you and Emily are getting along really well," Mom said.

"Yeah," I replied. "But, um, I was kind of jealous for a while. You act like she's perfect all the time. I was starting to think that you wanted me to be more like her or something."

"Oh, Katie!" Mom said, and her eyes got sad. "Let me concentrate on driving, but I promise you we'll finish this conversation."

I could tell that Mom was thinking hard on the whole ride home. When she pulled into our driveway, she shut the engine off and turned to look at me.

"Katie, you are my daughter, the love of my life, and I love you exactly as you are," Mom said. "Of course there are some habits that I would like you to improve, but that's my job as a parent."

I nodded. "Just maybe don't compare me to Emily when you do that."

Mom was shaking her head. "I never realized I was doing it, but now that you say it, you are so right. I'm sorry, Katie. I never wanted to make you feel bad about yourself."

"It's okay," I said. Boy, was it a relief to talk about stuff! And there was still one thing that was really bugging me. "Mom, if you marry Jeff—"

Mom interrupted me. "Katie, I am not sure if that will ever happen."

"I know, but I'm just saying, if you guys get married, I don't want to be the only Brown in the family," I said.

"What do you mean?" Mom asked.

"Well, if you take his name, you'd be Dr. Green," I pointed out. "And if you hyphenated your name, you'll be Dr. Brown-Green. And Emily would still be Emily Green, but I'd be Katie Brown. That would be sad."

Mom smiled. "Katie, that is a promise I can make. Okay?"

"Okay," I said, and I smiled back.

On Monday, everybody at school was talking about the talent show. At lunch George was juggling apples at his table, impressing all his friends.

"I heard that Olivia Allen is jealous of you," Emma reported to Alexis, "because everyone says you're a better singer."

Alexis shrugged. "I actually think she was really good. Anyway, people will stop talking about it soon."

"Well, Channel Eight aired their report last night," Mia said. "Did you see it?"

Alexis groaned. "My dad has played it, like, a million times. And they showed me for only two seconds."

"Two superstar seconds!" I teased.

"That reminds me," Alexis said. "Mary Chang e-mailed me and said they're going to air the Cupcake Club story on tomorrow's news. Mom said we could have pizza at our house and all watch it. I can't believe we're all going to be on TV!"

"Emily's in it, so I'll see if she can come too," I suggested, and everyone nodded.

The next day, we all got to Alexis's house at five. The news started at five thirty, and we wanted to make sure we didn't miss the Cupcake Club segment. Mrs. Becker had these little TV trays set up in the living room so we could eat our pizza without making a mess. We each had a huge stack of napkins, too.

At five thirty, the news came on. There was a story about the school budget and a store that got robbed. Then we saw Mary Chang's face on the screen.

"Coming up, hear about a group of girls who turned a love of cupcakes into a thriving business!" she said.

We all clapped and cheered. The commercials seemed to take forever. The show came back on, and the anchorman did a story about a new exhibit at the zoo. Then he turned things over to Mary Chang.

Suddenly, there we were on the screen—me, Mia, Emma, and Emily, setting up the cupcake table.

"Look at us!" Mia cried, and we all squealed. It was so weird seeing myself on TV. But I guess we looked pretty cool, since we all had our Cupcake shirts on.

Mary Chang started doing a voiceover.

"This might look like a typical school bake sale. But it's anything but," she was saying. "These girls have turned cupcakes into a booming business."

Emma's face appeared on the screen. "It started on our first day of middle school, when Katie brought a cupcake to lunch," she said.

Then the camera was right on me. "Lunch. School. Cupcake," I said.

"Oh no!" the non-TV me wailed. "Emma, I thought you said they were going to cut that out!"

"Shh!" Alexis said.

The rest of it was pretty normal, just like I'd remembered, with Emma and Mia talking. Then the camera turned to Mary Chang.

"One member, Alexis Becker, was too busy wowing the crowd in the talent show to be interviewed," she said. "Alexis is the business brain of the club, and she wanted me to make sure I gave out the club's website info. So check out the bottom of your screen if you want to give their cupcakes a try."

"Yes!" Alexis said, pumping her fist in the air.

The last shot they showed was a cute little kid biting into one of our cupcakes, and then the story was over. Everyone started talking at once.

"You guys looked so good!" Emily said.

131

"Alexis, you should have been in it," Emma said with a frown.

"It's okay," Alexis said. "I'm already a superstar, remember?"

"Excuse me, but did anybody hear what I dork I was?" I asked. "Why would she leave that in? It's like I forgot how to use the English language."

"It went by really fast," Mia assured me. "I'm sure nobody will notice."

Alexis's phone starting buzzing, and she looked at it. "No way! I already have a message about a possible birthday party order. Awesome!"

"Getting on the show was a brilliant idea," Emma told her.

Then my phone started to buzz. I looked at the screen. There was a text from George.

Lunch. School. Cupcake. ☺

"Oh no!" I wailed.

"What is it?" Mia asked.

I handed her my phone, and she started cracking up. Then everyone gathered around to look.

Emily started to giggle, and Mia and Emma were laughing really hard. Alexis had one of those "brilliant idea" looks that she gets.

"This could be great," she said. "We can isolate the clip and put it online. I bet we'd get a lot of hits. Then we could link to our Cupcake website."

"Absolutely not!" I shrieked. "If you do that, then I will post your singing clip on every website out there. You will be discovered and they'll make you go on tour and you won't be able to go to any more business club meetings."

Alexis frowned. "You wouldn't."

"I would!" I promised.

She sighed. "But it would be really good for business."

"I think we'll get enough business from the news report," I said.

"And if that doesn't work, we can add singing cupcake telegrams to our flyer," Emma said, looking at Alexis.

We all started laughing again. I looked around the room, and then I knew for sure—I might be starting from scratch, but I'd always have my friends around me to help me make sure everything came out perfect.

Want another sweet cupcake?

Here's a sneak peek

of the next book in the

CUPCAKE 🧁 DIARIES

series:

Mia's
recipe for
disaster

My Big Break!

"All right, people! Hit the lockers!" yelled out Ms. Chen, our gym teacher.

I jogged off the basketball court along with my friends Katie, Emma, and Alexis. We all have gym together, which is pretty nice. We all have pretty complicated feelings about gym, though.

Emma is blonde, sweet, a little shy, and gorgeous—and, surprisingly, a competitive beast when she plays sports. I think it comes from having three brothers. She especially gets mad when the girls and boys play together and the boys don't pass the ball to the girls.

"What do they think? That we're not as good as them?" she'd say.

Alexis is competitive, too, but mostly about academic things. She likes gym—mostly because she's really good at it—but she just loves to criticize it. "You need a healthy body to maintain a healthy mind," she'd always say. "But gym class is just not an efficient way to get exercise. Half the time we're standing around, waiting to play."

Then there's my best friend, Katie. She used to hate gym more than I hate polyester, mostly because she used to get teased because she wasn't good at sports. But she's a lot more confident now.

"Can you believe I made a basket today?" she was saying as we walked toward the locker room. She jumped up, pretending to make an imaginary layup. "An actual basket. In gym!"

"You did great, Katie," Emma said.

"I almost wish gym wasn't over yet," Katie said, and I gave her a look.

"Did you actually just say that?" I asked.

"Well, I said 'almost,'" Katie replied.

"Well, I am definitely glad it's over," I said. "That means I can get out of this uniform."

I am at war with my Park Street Middle School gym uniform. For one thing, it's half polyester, which is just itchy and gross. Polyester makes me sweat more, which is the exact opposite of what I need in a gym uniform. As Alexis would say, it's not logical.

Then there are the shorts, which balloon out on

the sides like old-fashion bloomers. And it's a totally boring blue color, not a deep navy or a pretty powder blue, but just this really dull blue, a dirty grayish blue, like the color of the sky on a drizzly day. Blah.

"Mia, you look great in the uniform," Katie said. "You look great in everything."

"Thanks, but nobody looks good in this," I said. I pulled at the fabric of the shorts. "I took these to my last class at Parsons, and Millicent, a design student, showed me how to alter the seam, so they don't look so baggy. But they're still hideous!" Parsons is a pretty famous design school in the city. My mom signed me up for classes there, which are totally awesome.

By now we had reached the locker room and quickly got changed for next period: lunch. We only get about three minutes to change, which is ridiculous. I never have time to redo my hair, which is always all over the place after gym.

"How is that class going, anyway?" Alexis asked.

"Really good," I said. "I'm learning so much about sewing. Which I'm going to need to do if I'm serious about becoming a fashion designer."

"Oh, you're definitely serious about it, all right," Katie said. "It's all you talk about."

"Not all," I said, but then I remembered

something. "Oh! I have something to show you guys at lunch. I found out about it yesterday, and I'm so excited!"

"Yesterday? Why didn't you tell me on the bus this morning?" Katie asked.

"I wanted to save it and tell everybody at lunch," I told her. "This could totally be my big break."

Katie raised her eyebrows. "Tell us now!"

"Not in this smelly locker room," I said, and then the bell rang. "Come on, let's go to lunch!"

The four of us pushed our way through a sea of middle schoolers as we headed to the cafeteria. Once we got there, Katie and I went to our usual table, and Alexis and Emma got on the food line.

"Come on, just tell me now," Katie said as she unwrapped her PB&J sandwich.

I shook my head. "You are so impatient!" I told her, laughing.

Katie put down her sandwich and closed her eyes. "Okay. I'll just meditate until you're ready, then."

That's when Alexis and Emma walked up, carrying trays of salad.

"What's with Katie?" Emma asked.

"I'm meditating," Katie said.

"Not if you're talking," I pointed out.

"Meditation can be very beneficial," Alexis said. "In business club we learned that many successful executives practice it. It keeps them focused."

Katie opened her eyes. "Okay, I'm focused. Now tell us, Mia!"

I opened my backpack and took out a magazine, *Teen Runway*. I flipped through the pages and stopped at a photo of a model gliding down a runway in a gorgeous chiffon evening gown. The headline above her read, "Design Your Fantasy Dress—Enter Our Contest!"

"*Teen Runway* is having a contest," I told my friends. "It's open to anyone between the ages of twelve and sixteen. You have to create a dress that you would wear to a fashion event with all the top designers. The top prize is a thousand bucks, but that's not even the best part. The winner gets their dress photographed on a professional model for the magazine, plus a meeting with famous designers."

I put the magazine down on the table, so everyone could see. "I can totally do this," I said. "Especially now that I'm taking those sewing classes. You have to sew your dress yourself and send in a picture of it for the contest."

"You can totally *win* this," Katie said, excited.

"Totally," Emma agreed, nodding.

"It's the perfect contest for you," Alexis said. "Although I wonder how many people will be competing. Do you know how many subscribers the magazine has? Maybe we could estimate."

"I think maybe it's better if you don't think about the other competitors," Emma suggested. "Just bring your amazing vision to life."

I nodded. "Exactly! On every fashion competition show I've watched, people get in trouble when they worry about what other people are doing."

"So can you do the sewing at your class in the city?" Katie asked.

"That's my plan," I said. "This week, I'm here with Mom. I can spend the time sketching and figuring out what material I need. Then next weekend I'm at Dad's, so I can work on the pattern there."

My parents are divorced, so every other weekend I take the train to New York City, where I used to live, and hang out with my dad. The rest of the time I live here in Maple Grove with my mom; my stepdad, Eddie; and Dan, my stepbrother. It used to be much more confusing, but we all figured it out, and now it just seems normal.

Katie scrunched up her face. "I almost forgot. Will you be around the weekend of George's Halloween party?"

"Yes. And even if I wasn't, I would ask Dad if I could go. I definitely don't want to miss that."

Suddenly, George Martinez appeared at our lunch table.

"So are you guys all going to dress up like cupcakes for my party?" he asked.

Katie almost jumped out of her chair. "George! We were just talking about you. That is so weird."

George waggled his eyebrows. "Really! Were you talking about how cute I am?"

Katie blushed, because she *does* think George is cute. Which is okay because he thinks Katie is cute, too. You can totally tell.

"No," she said. "We were talking about your party."

"And we are *not* going as cupcakes," I said. "That would be ridiculous." But I understood why George suggested it. My friends and I formed a cupcake club when we started middle school. We bake cupcakes for parties and other events. Everyone in school pretty much knows us as "the Cupcakers."

"Actually, it's a pretty cool idea," Katie said. "Although it might be kind of hard to go to the bathroom in a giant cupcake costume."

George laughed. "Yeah, right. But you're all coming, right?"

"Yes!" we all answered at once.

"Good," George said, and he headed back to his lunch table.

"*Everybody* is going to that party," Alexis said, leaning in toward us.

"I know," Emma said, her blue eyes shining. "The last time I went to a boy-girl party at somebody's house, it was, like, first grade or something."

Katie nudged me. "Is Chris going?"

Now it was my turn to blush. "I'm not sure," I said. "He hasn't texted me in a while."

Chris Howard is this boy in my grade who I'm pretty sure I like. He's tall and cute, and he has braces like I do, only mine are the clear kind, and he has the shiny metal kind. But they don't make him any less cute.

Emma was frowning. "I haven't thought about a costume yet. If we don't go as cupcakes, what will we go as?"

"If I didn't have this contest, I would design fabulous costumes for all of us," I said. "Sorry."

"No, the contest is way more important," Katie said, and Emma and Alexis nodded in agreement.

Then Alexis opened up her planner. "So, Cupcake Club meeting at your house, Mia? Saturday?"

I nodded. "Mom and Eddie said fine. We could

get pizza, or Eddie said he'd make spaghetti for us."

"Eddie's spaghetti!" Katie sang out. "It's delicious, and besides, it rhymes."

Alexis looked at the clock. "Ten minutes until the bell rings, and we haven't eaten a bite." She picked up her fork and dug into her salad.

I picked up my turkey wrap in one hand and stared at the magazine page in my other hand.

If I win this contest, it could change everything, I thought. *I could go from middle schooler to fashion designer overnight!*

Spooky Sketches

*W*hen I actually sat down to start sketching that night, creating my fantasy dress was way harder than I thought. What did it actually mean to make a "fantasy dress"? Should it be sophisticated, like something you'd wear to an art gallery opening, or runway-ready glamorous?

And even though I had said that I didn't want to worry about what other people might do, I *was* kind of worried. It was so hard to keep up with all the changing trends. Not that I wanted to follow them, but I knew I had to be ahead of them. My mom is a stylist, which means she helps pick out outfits and whole wardrobes for people. She helps magazines figure out which clothes to show, or she will help actresses with their wardrobes for a TV show or movie. She even styles "regular" people, too. It's pretty cool. Anyway, Mom was always talking about "being on trend," so I know it's important.

I opened up my laptop and started searching for the fall runway shows. My head was pretty much in Paris when Mom stepped in through the open doorway.

"Mia, did you finish your homework?" she asked.

"I just have one worksheet to do," I said, quickly closing the window on my screen so Mom wouldn't see the model in the slinky sequined gown. But she already had me figured out.

"Honey, I know you're excited about the contest, but school first, okay?"

I sighed. "Yes." I shut the laptop closed. But inside I was thinking, *If I win that contest, school won't matter!* Which, okay, to be honest, deep down I knew wasn't true, but it was still fun to dream.

I quickly finished my homework and then went back online. There were so many trends: hot pants with blazers, retro-looking dresses, lots of leather and fake fur. How was I supposed to come up with the *next* big thing?

As I flopped down onto my bed, Mom came back in.

"Bedtime, Mia. Laptop off, please."

"I know," I said, but I didn't move. I was too depressed. Mom sat down next to me.

"What's wrong?" she asked.

"I don't know how designers do it," I said. "How do you create something that nobody's ever done before and that everybody wants?"

Mom thought for a moment. She knows a lot of designers. "As a stylist, I listen to what my clients want and then try to find a designer who shares that same kind of style. Most designers have a specific style. The most successful ones have a style that appeals to a lot of people and that is wearable for a lot of people. I love leopard-print jumpsuits, but that is not something everyone can pull off."

I shuddered, imagining some of my friends' moms wearing leopard-print jumpsuits. "Yeah, not a good look for normal everyday wear."

"Talk to your friends," Mom suggested. "Find out what they would want in a fantasy dress. It may spark some ideas."

"That's a great idea!" I said, jumping up. I rooted under my bed and pulled out some fashion magazines from the stack that has piled up under there. Then I stuffed them into my backpack. "I can ask them at our Cupcake meeting on Saturday. Oh by the way, they want Eddie to make his spaghetti."

Mom smiled. "He'll be thrilled."

Mom said good night, and I got ready for bed. That night I dreamed I was walking down a runway, wearing my gym uniform, leopard-print boots, and a fake fur vest.

I can't believe I didn't wake up screaming!

Convincing my friends to help me out was easy. Well, I could tell that Katie *wanted* to give me a hard time. When I handed her some magazines to look through at lunch the next day, she looked at me like I was handing her a dirty sock.

"So you want us to do what?" she asked.

I handed her a purple marker. "Just look through it and circle the stuff you like. Stuff you might wear. You don't have to do it now—just bring it Saturday."

"Ooh, this is going to be fun!" Emma said.

"Are you sure you want *me* to do this?" Katie asked. Her idea of dressing up is to wear a clean pair of jeans with her T-shirt and sneakers. But once in a while she lets me pick out clothes for her, and she looks totally adorable.

"Yes, *you*," I insisted.

My friends didn't disappoint me. Saturday at five o'clock, the house smelled like tomato sauce and garlic, and when the doorbell rang, my dogs, Tiki and Milkshake, started yapping like crazy. When I opened the door, Katie, Emma, and Alexis were standing there, carrying the magazines I had given them.

They came inside, and Katie bent down to pet the dogs. They adore her.

"Emma, how was your modeling thing?" I asked. She gets professional modeling gigs sometimes.

"Another catalog," Emma said. "Winter coats. And it felt like ninety degrees in the studio. Gross!"

"Well, I got pretty sweaty during the race this morning," Katie said.

"Did your mom and Mr. Green run too?" I asked. Katie's mom is dating a math teacher, Mr. Green, in our school. It's really nice, but weird for Katie. Katie and her mom run, and Mr. Green does, too, so now they all run together sometimes.

"Yes, and Emily too," Katie said—Emily's Mr. Green's daughter—and grinned. "But I beat them all."

"So how do you want to do this?" Alexis asked. "Fashion first or cupcakes first?"

"Let's do fashion, then spaghetti, and then talk about cupcakes for dessert," Katie suggested. "It's, you know, fitting."

"Okay, let's go to my room," I said.

I had cleaned up my room (well, I shoved a few things under the bed), but I keep it pretty clean because I have loved it ever since Eddie helped me redo it. The walls are turquoise, and Eddie and I painted over the old furniture a glossy white, with black trim. Mom helped me with the colors but mostly it was my design.

I tossed some turquoise and fuchsia throw pillows from my bed to the floor.

"Okay, let's see what you've got," I told my friends.

"Me first!" Emma said, handing me a magazine. "I found tons of beautiful dresses in here."

I flipped through the pages. The dresses she had circled with the pink marker I gave her were—what else?—pink and fluffy, or they had floral prints.

"These are so *you*," I told her. "So, do you think 'romantic' would be a good way to describe your style? Or 'sweet and flirty'?"

Emma nodded. "Definitely," she said, looking down at the white peasant top and pink skirt she was wearing.

"Well, I didn't circle anything with flowers," Alexis said. She handed me back the stack of magazines I had given her, with the pages neatly flagged.

"The ones I liked best looked nice, but they were practical, too."

Katie frowned. "You mean like uniforms?"

"No, I mean—well, turn to page thirty-seven of that one," Alexis said, pointing, and I quickly obeyed. "See that black dress? You can wear it to work during the day, and then you can dress it up and wear it to a party at night. It says it right here: 'One dress, two different looks, pretty and practical!'"

I nodded. "My mom's clients love stuff like that."

Then I looked at Katie. "Sooooo . . ."

Katie sighed and handed me the magazines. "Well, I didn't find my fantasy dress. I found some stuff I wouldn't mind wearing, though."

Looking through the pages, I saw that Katie circled a lot of pictures of models wearing jeans and shirts, or shorts and shirts. No surprise there.

"Well, what would your fantasy dress look like?" I asked.

"I was thinking about that," Katie said. "I guess if I had a really special thing to go to, I would want something completely different and amazing. Like a dress with a rainbow swirl all around it, or maybe a silver space-looking dress with a hat that had spirals coming out of it."

Alexis laughed. "I could so see you in that!"

"I tried to draw it, but it came out terrible," Katie said.

But I was already sketching. After a minute I held out my sketch pad to Katie.

"Like this?" I asked.

Katie looked at my drawing, which showed a sleeveless dress that was short in the front and long in the back. The hat on the figure I had drawn was a small cap topped with a twisting spiral, kind of like what DNA looks like.

Katie's brown eyes lit up. "That is awesome!"

"I think it might be too ... creative for this contest," I said. "But it's really fun. I will totally design that for you someday."

"You'd better!" Katie said.

Then we heard Eddie's voice call up the stairs. "Who wants some of Eddie's spaghetti?"

"Meeeee!" Katie yelled back, and she raced out of the room ahead of all of us.

The spaghetti smelled delicious, but I could barely eat. My head was filled with ideas for the perfect dress. I was going to win this contest!

Coco Simon always dreamed of opening a cupcake bakery but was afraid she would eat all of the profits. When she's not daydreaming about cupcakes, Coco edits children's books and has written close to one hundred books for children, tweens, and young adults, which is a lot less than the number of cupcakes she's eaten. Cupcake Diaries is the first time Coco has mixed her love of cupcakes with writing.

Want more

CUPCAKE DIARIES?

Visit **CupcakeDiariesBooks.com**
for the series trailer, excerpts, activities,
and everything you need for throwing
your own cupcake party!

Still Hungry?

There's always room for another Cupcake!

Katie and the
Cupcake Cure

1

Mia in the Mix

2

Emma on Thin Icing
3

Alexis and the
Perfect Recipe
4

Katie, Batter Up!

5

Mia's Baker's Dozen
6

Emma All Stirred Up!
7

Alexis
Cool as a Cupcake
8

Katie and the
Cupcake War
9

Mia's Boiling Point

10

Emma, Smile and
Say "Cupcake!"

11

Alexis Gets Frosted
12

Katie's New Recipe
13

Mia a Matter of Taste
14

Emma Sugar and Spice and Everything Nice
15

Alexis and the Missing Ingredient
16

Katie Sprinkles & Surprises
17

Mia Fashion Plates and Cupcakes
18

Emma: Lights! Camera! Cupcakes!
19

Alexis the Icing on the Cupcake
20

Katie Starting from Scratch
21

Mia's Recipe for Disaster
22

If you liked

CUPCAKE 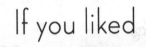 DIARIES

be sure to check out these

other series from

Simon Spotlight

SIMON   **KEN**
Simon, Coco.
Katie starting from scratch /

KENDALL
06/23